ORANGE

THE DIARY OF AN URBAN SURREALIST

A novelzine by
Stephen Janis

Published by Novelzine, Baltimore, MD

Layout/Design: Michael Hilton

Cover Photo: Justin Sirois

Inside Photos: Frank Klein

Edited by Taya Graham

ORANGE

TABLE OF CONTENTS

YESTERDAY

PART ONE

—Orange. Paula says.
She divides the mattress in half with her large frame. I nudge her in
the back with my knee.

—Orange. She repeats.

I sit up on the edge of the bed and light a cigarette. The match falls
to the floor. It singes the tip of my new leather slipper. I'm awake,
it's too early, but I am awake. Paula rolls to my side of the futon,
swinging one her overdeveloped calves into my ass.

Walking to the bathroom, past the window, I see snow. The entire
park is white. Maybe the whole city is fucking frozen. Stepping
into the bathroom, the floor is ice cold.

Already undressed, I prepare to shower. Turn the hot water faucet,
nothing happens. Wrench it around in a full circle, nothing happens. Pick up the bottle of herbal shampoo and drip a spot into my
hand.

—Orange

As her voice echoes in the bathroom, the walls start to shake.
Overloaded with water, the tiles ripple back and forth. A seismic
wave tosses me into the bathtub.

—Orange...

Sitting in the tub dazed, the shaking continues. The shower fixture rattles. A purple mist bleeds between the cracks of broken bath tiles. A colored liquid drips from the ceiling, flowing down the walls. The nozzle erupts, spewing the entire spectrum, covering my body with paint.

I close my eyes; the substance flows over me. My body is covered, head to toe. It tastes like water, odorless. The bathtub is filling up, rising. Crossing my legs back and forth I try to get up, try to right myself. I grab the side of the tub and pull my trunk over the edge, falling, hitting my back on the bathroom floor and rolling into the corner.

Huddled on the floor, the deluge spreads to all the cracks and crevices in the bathroom. I curl up into a ball and wait. The floor is covered an inch thick, and the stuff is rising. I am paralyzed. My head throbs with migraine-like pain, I drift off into semi-consciousness as Paula yells again:
—ORANGE!....

A bar, unfamiliar, filled with time tourists, sketchy fabric, baked wallpaper. The clock on the wall said 6:30. The man sitting next to me was old, black and half-asleep. He slapped me on the back.
—Wake-up, it's only six thirty.
—I can't stay awake...beer makes me tired.
—Local beer's got lead in it — he laughed.
—So I've heard.

Too much cigarette smoke, I couldn't see his face, only his lips, tapering glow worms. I was confused; the clock still said 6:30. I asked:
—Do I know you?
—Don't you fucking remember me? He laughed.
I answered No.
—I'm the cab driver.
—Cab driver?
—The train station...remember?
—I don't remember...anything, fucking nothing

The clock on the wall said 6:30.

A train leaves a station, it goes underground, into a tunnel...I rode it
from New York to this city, it arrived at 4 a.m. The station was
empty. The cavernous ceilings absorbed my footsteps as I walked
into the spare light of near dawn.

I got in the only cab parked in front of the station. The cab driver
had one arm. I lit a cigarette as we sped through an intersection
and down a four-lane causeway (over a river, I think).

We drove past a dozen hollow office buildings. Turned down a narrow side street stamped with potholes. I saw a decomposed 7-11
with plywood windows. Up a small hill the city unrolled like an
internment camp as the rising sun swept the top of the archaic sky-
line. The cab driver stopped, turned around.
—Where are you going?
—1105 Callet Street.
—I know a short cut.
We took a sharp turn into a back alley and then cut across a few
street corners. The cab bounced like a speedboat on a concrete
wake.
—Could you slow down, it's like turbulence in a fucking trashcan.
The driver stopped the cab, eyeing me in the rear view mirror.
—Not in this fucking neighborhood.
—I'm not in a hurry; it's five o'clock in the fucking morning.
The driver stepped on the gas. He drove with his left arm, his only
arm.

—You on vacation?

—I'm moving here, from New York.

—You left New York for this rat hole?

—I don't know, I remember taking a shower, and then getting on a train.

—Shit...everyone's moving out, you're moving in.

We stopped in front of a red brick row house on Callet. A tiny old woman ran from across the street waving her arms. She was frail, her hands trembled, and she had a quarter-sized mole sprouting hair in the middle of her forehead.

—You got any money? She asked as I got out of the cab.

—I'm broke.

—I'll carry your bags.

—C'mon lady, I just fucking got here.

I walked up the stoop of 1105.

It was the address of a friend I'd met when I lived in Kingston. He moved here, following a woman named Marcia.

I walked through the front hall and up an old wood staircase. On the third floor landing was apartment 3b, his. I knocked on the door and waited...no answer. I knocked again, no answer. I twisted the door knob and entered.

The apartment was empty. A ratty black leather couch sat in the middle of a large open room. An empty fireplace was filled with a skeletal space heater. The kitchen smelled like natural gas and was littered with dead cockroaches.

In the main room, a TV and VCR were stacked on top of a cinder block. The bedroom was empty except for a plastic milk crate filled with jumper cables. Paint peeling from the unnaturally high ceilings dropped to the floor like lead leaves.

I threw my suitcase on the floor and opened the one large window in the center of the living room.

A tall wiry woman stood on the sidewalk across the street. Large gold hoop earrings dropped from a full red Afro. She wore a skin-tight Lycra body stocking. Her legs were tapered and feminine set against broad, muscular shoulders. I lit a cigarette, sat down on the couch and fell asleep.

I woke up short of breath. Rolled off from the couch, I walked to
the window. Callet Street was empty. I backpeddled into the
kitchen; outside the window was a fire escape. Through the window
I saw a building that looked like prison.

Set back to the left of the prison, was a high-rise hospital. A large
fluorescent caduceus dangled from the roof like a monstrous snake.

I became nauseous. I gripped the bottom of the window and tried
to open it. It wouldn't budge. I pushed again. It moved a centime-
ter. Got up underneath and pushed with my legs. The window
opened, and I stepped out onto the fire escape.
—I thought you weren't coming back?
...it was Paula, sitting on the edge of a fold-out futon in our apart-
ment. The plaster light made her hair look blonder, her face tan
and sun aged.
—What are you talking about Paula?
—You left without saying anything
Light, hollow afternoon grist migrated up and down the bedroom of
our apartment.
—Well I've slept better since you left she said.
—So you're not pissed off?
She laughed. —I really didn't miss you, in bed anyway.
Paula sat down on the floor next to me. She touched my nose with
her fingertips.
—Do you have a cigarette?

—Sure. I stuck a Marlboro in her mouth, she touched my face again.

—It feels like you've been gone a long time

—Do you remember when I left?

—No. She laid on the floor, dragging off the cigarette. —Could you fix the window, I think it's stuck?

—I'll check it out.

She pointed at the large bay window; I undid the latch and pushed it from the bottom. It was stuck. I got up under it and pushed with my legs. Lifting for a few seconds, it opened a crack, but then I was dizzy again.

I woke up on the fire escape. The air was thick as plastic. The sun looked green behind a sheet of phosphorous clouds. Grabbing the iron bars covering the kitchen window, I pulled hard, searching for a weak spot. Pushing the gate far enough apart, I crawled through the small hole I'd made and back into the apartment.

1 : 0 2 : 0 2 : 0 2

The sidewalk felt like quicksand in the heat. I stepped forward and my foot sunk. Walking to the store to get cigarettes, a sudden thunderstorm bent the gutted row houses in half. Underneath sheets of rain, I ran all the way back to the apartment.

Toweling off in the bathroom, my face looked odd. I was white, off white, pale as death. I could be twenty, or thirty; it's hard to tell. I'm fairly ugly; my nose is scarred and too long, dividing my face into an concoction of angles and flesh.

Underneath the kitchen sink, I found an old bottle of rum. Appleton's Estate, a souvenir my friend had brought from Kingston. I opened the freezer, found some ice and poured a glass into a paper cup.

I got the Xanax out of my suitcase. I stole it from Paula, who had borrowed it from a friend who, I don't know, maybe got it from a psychiatrist. Paula used it for panic attacks. Crushing the pills with the stem of a dusty wineglass, I sprinkled the powder in my drink, laying down on the couch for a quick nap.

A while later, maybe an hour, I heard noises coming from the kitchen. I crept around the corner of the open doorway just off the living room.

My father stood by the sink holding the bottle of Appleton's. He looked pale but still strong. Heavy set with a wave of black hair. Speaking to him for the first time since he died, I asked:

—Am I dreaming?

He turned around, holding the bottle of Appleton's. He was slightly off white, but still much healthier than the liquored ghost I expected. He asked:

—How much of this stuff have you drank already?

—There was about a quarter bottle left when I started.

He raised his glass. —Here, or in the living room?

—I don't care.

He walked out of the kitchen and sat on the end of the couch. He sipped his drink without speaking, the contours of his face smooth and elastic in the semi-darkness of late afternoon. Finally he spoke...

—This apartment is empty son.

—I don't think my friend lives here anymore.

—It isn't yours?

—No.

—Do you have your own place?

Lifting the glass, he finished off a shot. I asked:

—Why are you here?

—You tell me son.

—I don't know, I fell asleep then you appear.

—You know what they say about the dead.

—No.

—Gone but not forgotten.

Gone but not forgotten...

He laughed, raising his glass high in the air before finishing it off. I fell asleep before the bottle was empty.

I woke up; the apartment was dead quiet. It was raining, a vicious rain that coats the windows so you can't see a thing.

Retrieving the small portable stereo I had given Paula for her birthday from my suitcase, I placed it in the corner next to the window. Loading it with the only CD brought from New York, I turned up the volume and lay on the floor.

Someone pounded on the door; I opened it. A man, linguini-like hair and dark half-moon circles under his eyes stood in the hallway. There was a *Tech Nine* automatic pistol wedged under his belt.
—Who the fuck are you? He demanded.
—I'm a visitor.
—Visiting who?
—My friend, he lives here.
—That guy moved out a month ago.
The gun was sparkling, throwing off platelets of light, making me dizzy.
—I don't really care if you want to squat, just turn the fucking music down.
—What's with the gun?
—I always carry a gun....you like it?
—Yeah, it's beautiful.
—Check this out...
He pointed the gun behind his back and shot off a round, staring at me as the bullet dissected the chandelier, scattering glass shrapnel into a twilight wake. He turned the gun around, aimed it at the ceil-

ing, and shot off two more rounds. The bullets splintered the banister, sending flakes of sawdust floating in the air like angel's dust.

Finished, he stepped inside the front door, gun still drawn, pointed at me.
—Isn't it kind of weird, living in an empty apartment?
—Yeah. You want a drink?
—Want my advice?
—No.
—Buy a gun.
—Okay.
—Give yourself a week or two, you'll be begging me for one.

He stepped outside the door, pushing the *Tech Nine* through his belt and into his crotch. Walking down the spiral staircase, I watched him stroke the sleek, metallic weapon, as if it were a baby. When I heard the door to his apartment close, I retreated to the couch and went to sleep.

I found an old television set in the back of the bedroom closet. It was so retro it didn't have a video input or stereo outputs. The small silicon-coated speaker was pushed inside out.

I turned it on, flipped through the channels. It only picked up one station, which seemed to be running infomercials and promotional pitches for insect care.

Suddenly the apartment shook so violently I was thrown off the couch. I got up, walked to the window and looked out.

A large Wiederman's beer truck was driving up Callet. The old woman intercepted the truck, running alongside until she jumped, hitching a ride on the driver's side door.

The truck stopped and a man in a dark green sleeveless shirt got out. He dragged the woman across the street, rolling her over on the sidewalk. She lay flat on the ground, flapping her arms up and down like a dazed insect.

The front door opened and closed. Someone pulled my legs off the couch, grabbed my shoulders, then slapped me across the face.
—Wake up man, wake up...Wake the fuck up! WAKE UP!!

Feeling nauseous and sweaty, I opened my eyes to see my friend standing over me, his white head shining in the late afternoon light.
—Wake up GODDAMNIT! Wake up!

I rolled off the couch and fell onto the floor. My friend's face was twisted and covered with sweat — malignant.
—What the hell are you doing here, I thought you lived in New York? – He yelled.
—I was asleep.
—I got a call from the guy downstairs, said someone's living in my old apartment...I didn't expect it to be you!!!
—You said to stop by anytime, I had this address.
He pulled a cell phone out of his shirt pocket.
—I have to call Marcia. *Yeah, he's here...I don't know honey, he had my address...He looks pretty clean.*
He hung up the phone, folding it into a square.
—Got any plans, other than getting out of here?
—Get a job, see what happens.
—Where the fuck are you going to live?
—Here.
—Are you nuts, I don't live HERE anymore.
My friend left me sitting on the couch and ran into the kitchen.

—I see you found the last bottle of rum.

He was angry, but he was always angry. Since the day I met him in Kingston, he did three hundred sit-ups every morning, punitive sit-ups, from every possible excruciating angle. His stomach muscles were tightly wound knots. He was meticulously clean and pale. He over-styled his hair to compensate for its loss.

I walked into the bathroom to wash up, put my head under the hot water in the bathroom sink, then brushed my teeth. Turbulent, deep blue circles churned under my eyes.

My friend was sitting on the couch reading a faded copy of the Financial Times, waiting for me. His eyes shifted from the paper to me, back to the paper, then again to me. He started talking before I could speak...

—I just can't fucking believe you think you're going to squat.

—Why fucking not? Better here than there.

My friend looked down at the floor and picked at his nose.

—What about the money I lent you in Kingston, for the beer...did you bring that?

I had it but didn't want to pay now.

—Can it wait? I'm a little short.

—I don't want to wait.

—How much was it?

—Five hundred.

—Half now, half when I get a job?

—How about all now, it's been five months.

I placed my wallet in his outstretched, trembling hands. He took out a clean roll of bills, stuffing them into his shirt pocket, before flipping the wallet back at me.

—Find a fucking place to live.

As he walked out of the apartment, the crisp clean lines of his corduroys fluffed like the ruffled feathers of a dull-colored bird.

Out the door, I heard him stomp down the stairs like a boot camp acolyte. As the door slammed, I made a wish that he would never return and I would be left alone to sleep as much as I fucking wanted.

I turned on the old TV. A commercial promoting city tourism fea-
tured a man and a woman wearing matching pale NikePro suits
walking on a sidewalk near the harbor.
The voiceover:

This city, imagine yourself here.
Or

This city, beyond your imagination.

Taking a whack at it myself I reworked the line to read:

This city, you're imagining it.

I left the apartment using a map my friend drew on the back of nap-
kin to look for a job thinking:

This city is imaginary.

Walked through an overgrown park past a bus stop sign painted
DISCONTINUED, then crossed the street and cut through an
empty parking lot. Scattered pieces of brightly colored plastic that
looked like malformed mollusks stuck to the treads of my shoes.

Crossed a deserted four-lane highway, through the lot of a gas station with cannibalized pumps. An old man sat in a booth smoking a

cigarette. He was reading a piece of paper shredded at the bottom. His eyes were fixated on the shredded part.

Ten blocks down Pullet street I reached the Midtown Renaissance Center, a cluster of four ultra-modern skyscrapers connected by parkways and giant pneumatic sculpture gardens.

It was the address of the largest ad in the paper:
TEMPS WANTED, WARM BODIES, HEALTHY MINDS.
Renaissance Tower One, 25th-floor offices of Perma Temp

The reception area was empty. A woman sat behind a credenza, her hair close-cropped bleach-bond offset by tiny blue eye slats. The rose tattoo on the side of her left cheek bloomed as she yelled before I closed the door:
—Don't slam the door before I push the buzzer!

I waited by the door. She reached under her desk. A high pitched buzzing sound resonated up and down the seams of the frame. I slowly turned the handle and pulled it closed.
—Thank you. She said.

She looked nervous; shuffling a pen like a cocktail mixer, licking a piece of gum stuck between her teeth.
—I want to apply for a job.
—Write your name on the sign-in sheet and take the WordPro test.

I waited for forty-five minutes.

Finally, a tall man with a cylindrical nose grabbed me by the arm and walked me to his office. He sat down on a sofa, then directed me to sit on a love seat. The office was filled with antique furniture and a long line of digital clocks keeping time for cities like London, Paris, and Rome. He talked fast:

—*If you want to be a good temporary, don't think temporarily. In other words, our "contractors" do not think like temps and don't act like temps. We provide our clients with a full-time simulation of a real time employee. Part-time workers contribute more to the real growth of the GDP than any other part of the work force.*

I interrupted to ask, —Real time?

—*Real Time is our industry's shorthand for full-time. There are real timers and simul timers, simul timers being you. It sounds like a lot of unnecessary jargon, but it's important that you understand the difference. This is an easy shorthand way to remember your role in the larger picture of what we like to call "the economy of flexible opportunity."*

—I've got it.

—Good. Let's take a look at your WordPro test.

Hypnotized by the puppet-like movements of his mouth, I nodded off. It was a poorly timed nap. I was dreaming again, talking to my father, or not sure...

—How could you sleep through a fucking interview?

—It's his fault not mine.

—You can't expect to get ahead by sleeping son.

A cold hand slapped me on the top of my head. My WordPro test was sitting on the table. My interviewer scratched his nose and checked his watch.

—Okay, read the PermaTemp employee manual and cut your hair.

He walked me to the door of the reception area. I took the elevator to the lobby and walked to Cassava Street.

Two blocks from the Renaissance Towers, his plain voice still echoed through the city.

I stood alone on Sherot Avenue waiting for the bus. The heat had risen beyond oppressive to unbearable. The bus was late. I fell asleep on a bench. When I woke up, it was dark.

0 2 : 2 7 : 1 4 : 0 7

I was employed, and although it seemed anticlimactic, I wanted to celebrate by sleeping again. As I stretched out on the couch, a phone rang.

At first I ignored it, burying my head into the folds of a rank pillow. But after several minutes, I realized that if I didn't answer the phone would keep me awake forever.

I ran around the apartment as long as it took me to find it. I searched the living room, the kitchen, the bathroom. Finally, stuck in the corner of a closet in the bedroom, hooked up by a cable that ran through the ceiling, I found an old black rotary phone. I answered it.
—What?
—Yeah, it's me.
—Who the fuck is me? (I asked)
—The guy downstairs, with the gun.
—What do you want?
—You seem kind of out of it
—Yeah, I was kind of asleep.
—Have you been taking anything?
—I've been drinking
—I've got all sorts of shit that could help.
—Yeah.
—I'm a mood agent...and you could use a little more brain activity.
—Sure, but I can't afford it.

—The first time is free; if it works…made to order, pharmaceutical Sushi.

My Tech Nine–toting neighbor was up the stairs and through the front door by the time I hung up the phone. He sat down the couch, opened a small silver flight case and removed half a dozen prescription bottles, setting them out on the floor in a row.

Meditating for several minutes, he licked his lips then quickly, like a Black Jack dealer, shuffled a few script bottles, unscrewed the caps with one hand, and dropped some pills into a coffee cup. Getting a pestle out of the suitcase, he ground the pills into fine powder, poured the powder into a glass, and shoved it across the table.
—Wash it down with something.
—What is it?
—It's my own creation, Mescan2.
—Will I wake up?
—So what if you fucking don't?

Mescan2 was a grainy white powder. Pouring the last drop of my friend's rum into a cup, I drank it down with a shot. A minute later I was asleep on the couch.

Waking up, I saw my father again, this time sipping a Coke. We sat in the kitchen next to the window, but the backdrop had shifted down-spectrum. He was self-consciously ghoulish. He spoke first.
—What a grainy city.
—I haven't seen the sun since I got here.
—You need a job son
—I have one.
My father laughed, hollow and right from the gut. —A temp job?

My son, the fucking temp.

—Even in my dreams you're an asshole.

—Are you sure they're yours, son? Are you sure?

—I'm sure you're more of an asshole dead than alive

He laughed like a Slovene devil.

—Are you sure son?

The dream ended in the afternoon. I woke up hungry and alert.

Walking down Callet, "For Sale" signs are in full bloom. A little hit of Mescan2 and I'm counting them like they're "hello" mushrooms. Not that these rusted, real-estate emblems are beautiful; it's just that block after block is for sale, so I call them city foliage.

I feel the urge to move myself in the opposite direction that everyone seems to be going: downtown. Is that the best move? I wonder. It all seems transparent, but maybe I'll hold out, and the city will become my private place, a communicable playground.

I count the moving vans and the mountains of splintered furniture piled on the sidewalk. The evictions take root in the spring and everyone will be gone except me. I realize, and it is a sudden realization, that my father is here too. That's the key, he's here but why...? If I knew maybe I could figure out why Paula still speaks to me, or how I ended up in this city at the end of train ride I don't remember.

Either way, I'm sure it's not just a minor, viral confusion that will be resolved before this ends, or I come to an alternate conclusion.

The phone rang, and I couldn't get off the couch. I was half-asleep,
as I twisted my shoulders toward the floor and dropped on my back.
I stumbled to the closet and picked it the receiver.
—What?
—How's the stuff? – (It was my dealer)
—My head's embalmed.
—Try it again, it gets easier, the buzz gets smoother.
—How much?
—Five bucks for two hits.
—Okay.

I had a job or an assignment. I remember washing my face and
brushing my teeth. I placed a small clock radio on the sink in the
bathroom and listened to the news, or the voice of the man who
reads the news. I remember taking a bus to the address written on
the back of an index card
—Do you know how to use...? The sweet smelling woman with a
ferocious smile asked.
—Yes. I answered.
She was sweating, drops of perspiration coiled around the base of
her neck.
—Are you familiar with...?
—Yes.
—Let me finish.
—Yes.
—Are you listening? Another devastating smile, golden brown hair,
warm ruts under her eyes.

—Yes.

—You're anticipating...

—I'm in a hurry.

—Why?

—I don't know.

I think she was staring at me. I smiled. —*I don't know, but I have the feeling the only answer I can give you today is yes... which is okay, as long as you're willing to accept yes as a definitive answer. The only problem is that I will probably say yes before you have a chance to finish your next question, which may or may not satisfy your demand for an answer.*

She picked up a pen off my desk and walked away before I could say yes again.

I was home later that evening, sorting through an old deck of cards.
The door opened and my friend threw a suitcase across the living
room.
—Don't say a fucking word.
—Okay.
—That's exactly what I don't want you to say.
Sweat dripped from behind his ears. Slit lips tight as ropes.
—I brought some beer with me.
He pulled a six pack out of the suitcase and walked into the kitchen.
He came back into the living room and sat down on the floor, beer
in hand.
I asked, —Can I have a beer?
—Sure.
He sat down on the couch and handed me a beer. We drank in
complete silence, falling asleep on opposite ends of his piece of dis-
carded furniture.

My friend stood in front of a body-length mirror. As far as I could tell he had moved in, waking in the morning before I did, and saying nothing about why he came back to the apartment.

I watched from the couch as he dressed in the empty bedroom. His tie was silver, his suit an acetone blue, sleek and linear. His hand pasted the few remnants of his hair onto the left side of his head in a gummy part.
—Where'd you find the mirror?
My friend turned around.
—It's your fucking fault.
—My fault?
Fidgeting with his collar, his teeth bared like a dog.
—You think this is a coincidence, you show up and now I'm here?
—What the fuck are you talking about?
—Go back to New York; stop fucking up my life.
Before I could answer, he marched out of the apartment, slamming the front door for effect.

—Fuck off! Somebody yelled from the street.

A gunshot rang slightly off key. Shrieking rubber tires of a braking car led to the mesh of metal with coughing sounds.

Remnants of daylight trickled past the frozen clock. The third floor cat clawed at the door so I let her in to eat leftover Chinese food.

The dealer's stereo blasted through the floorboards, rowdy metal churning of polyester bass colors. I poured a glass of white wine in a beer mug. A tiny pill rested on the tip of my index finger like a dotted orange candy corn. Popped in my mouth, it was bitter, rolling down my throat on a river of wine.

Truck engines rattled the glass of the living room. Fading into semiconscious sleep, I felt Paula next to me, whispering into my ear...*you can't leave sweetheart, you'll never get out...unless you can get rid of him....c'mon honey, figure it out....keep your eyes on the sun...*

A persistent dealer is a strange luxury. Even if the additive properties haven't taken over your body, even without cravings, a dealer
that won't give up can always accelerate the process into a steadily
deteriorating state of been gone.

Mescan2 smoothed out the ripples of the day, between a temp job
and my friend stomping around the apartment like a prison guard.
The phone rings.
—No credit, you understand?
—Who the fuck is this?
—The guy downstairs, with the gun.
—I just woke up.
—Pay me.
—I got it.
—You're in for about forty.
—I said I've got it. I've got it...plus twenty more.
—I'll be up in a minute.
A new glass stereo sits on the floor by the window; my friend sal-
vaged it from Marcia's place and set it up in the apartment to listen
to the news. He disemboweled the tuning knob so I can't change
stations or turn it down. I have to listen to monotonous news or
popular jazz all day long if I decide not to go to work.

But his plan doesn't change my plans. Mescan2 was prime insula-
tion. I will continue to sleep, drink, and buy. I have enough money
to support habit and permanent banks of clouds outside an empty
apartment to seed my dreams and keep my father at bay.

TODAY
PART TWO

I was talking to a fly. He had been sitting on the left arm of the couch since the day I had moved into the apartment. We started up a conversation based on a mutual hatred of my friend.

The Fly was generally quiet. If he did make a noise, I could translate it into human. It was always high pitched and modulated, sort of an incontinent melody. I asked him:
—Do you think this guy is a fucking idiot?
I pointed to my friend, who was lying on the floor reading the paper.
I thought the fly said, —I don't know, but his blood needs seasoning.
—You don't have to move, because I'm staying.
I thought he said, —Good looking out.

My friend posed in front of the mirror. He wore a bright suit, but the apartment was so dark he melted into the shadows of the empty bedroom, coming out like a fluorescent pallbearer. A soft spray of rain drifted through the hole in the living room window. I said:
—Have a drink with me before you leave.
—I can't.
—Just one, you'll feel better, confident.
—I don't want one.
—Big moments require antidotes.
He loitered in the living room, staring at the ceiling.
—Okay, just one.

—Got it.

I was in the kitchen quickly sorting through the glasses I had mixed that morning and stored in the refrigerator. Back in the living room, I handed him the glass.

—Here.

He took the glass from me and studied it. —What is it?

—A completely original drink.

He took a long hit.

—It's too sweet...I can't taste the alcohol.

—I didn't say anything about alcohol.

—This isn't bad, what's in it.

—I couldn't tell you even if I remembered

—I like it. Give me another.

After finishing his second drink, my friend sat on the couch, staring at the empty glass. I asked:

—Are you coming back, after the date?

—What the fuck do you care?

—I'd like to get some uninterrupted sleep

—Whatever.

My friend stood up, tried to straighten his back, fix his suit. He looked disjointed, a little wobbly.

—You looked relaxed now – I said

—I feel...okay.

—Suave, not stable.

—I feel pretty smooth, thanks for the drink.

—No problem.

My friend stumbled out the door. Seconds later, I heard a loud crash, the shattering of glass, and a string of expletives.

A few minutes later, sure he was gone, I slipped the last batch of Mescan2 into my drink, waiting on the couch in a waking coma for

my father to appear. He did, but I was too drunk to remember
what he said.

I ate a bad turkey sandwich at the Shoehorn Deli while I thought about my father. Getting rid of him would be easy, if my dealer would cooperate. It was a typical us-versus-them scenario (that is, the dead versus the living), which is fucked up if you think about it in the context of a single I.

The week-old salad bar of beige bowls filled with molted lettuce and tarnished green onions tasted bacterially confused. I felt sick, so I caught a cab home. As my stomach churned in the back of the cab, I watched as a thin man, hands stuffed in his dark windbreaker, smashed a car window, dove into the front seat, and emerged with a handful of CDs.

I went home, threw up in the bathroom, then dropped on the couch. Just as I fell asleep the phone rang.
—Hello?
It was a recording: —*Hello, this is the PermaTemp voice-activated dispatch system. You have an assignment at 1123 Callet Street, Barnable Associates, Third Floor. If you can accept this assignment please say yes after the tone....*

The keyboard felt dry under my trembling hands. The phone rang. I said, —Good morning, Mr. Strazza's office.

The coffee maker was larger than the copy machine. Mr. Strazza used a bowl instead of a regular cup. He smiled as I stood in front of his sleek rectangular desk. His PA grabbed my hand and walked me back to the coffee maker.
—He drinks a lot of coffee, she says, eight bowls a day.

We returned to the office with another bowl and Mr. Strazza was still smiling, but his lips were blue, arms outstretched, palms flat. A flash-freeze laugh crafted in plastic skin. His head rested stiffly on the straight-back leather chair.

The PA shook his shoulders, squeezed his hands, and screamed. Mr. Strazza is ultra-caffinated, or is he dead? An overdose of Mocha Rose and his stiff, onion eyes are offset by the broad, alert smile of man ready to face the challenges of a new business day except that...he's dead, stiff, unresponsive, unfriendly, unnetworkable, and unmanageable.

The phone rang as his PA screamed in a high falsetto, filling the office with operatic agony. Walking to my desk, I remained calm, answering the phone:
—Good morning, Mr. Strazza's office, officio, *Senor Strazza esta Muetro...*

The next night everything clicked. I mourned for Mr. Strazza by
cooking up sauces, a little blend of the Mescan2 and a few leftovers
from Paula, shooting it down in an overcharged minute.

I walked down Callet, actually rolled like a moldy tennis ball. I
mounted the black marble horse statue raised in the middle of an
ancient plot of grass boxed in by intersecting streets and wrought
iron gates, charging at the heroin addicts laid out on the grass who
barely raised their heads to curse me: the new Generalisimo of the
Park.
—Out...out, all of you...RISE!

The effect was minimal. If there had been a spare needle amongst
them, it would have landed in my back.

After my victory I left the park to get some food. I fondled the
sweating fronds of a plastic palm tree at the supermarket. Rolling
across the sidewalk with a bag of groceries, I fell into a haystack full
of needles. Injecting my body with warm, metallurgic fluids, I sat
on the fire escape and watched the decomposing trucks rust on an
abandoned off ramp.
Then I went to sleep.
The phone rings.
—What?
—Hey, this morning, on the fire escape, you looked like a zombie.
—I can't fucking sleep.

—Too much of the same stuff?

—Fuck the stuff - I just can't sleep.

—I have something, all the necessary corrective chemicals.

—Like what?

—A real smooth sedative, Electravite...like injecting twelve martinis straight into the pituitary gland...I mean, man this stuff is...

I fell asleep before he could finish, or at least, *it seemed that's how it seemed.*

The next morning my friend returned, and I could tell by the way he launched his suitcase, a long hurl from the living room into the bedroom that she'd given him the stock answer: no. I waited a few hours, reading a comic book I found in the alley while he ate a bowl of cereal.

He sat down next to me on the couch, cradling a magazine in his trembling hands.
—Marcia has a genetic problem.
—What are you talking about?
—Personality is almost all determined by genetics.
—Yeah?
—I'm reading right now so I understand.
He read to me from an article in a magazine called Personal Science.

—*The brain cultivates a natural entropy, an ongoing calibration between the properties of billions of cells, manifested in the electrical pulses, and organic supra instructions that determine the basic operative schema of the neural net. The palliative often described as personality is simply the indecipherable and underlying algorithmic equations that determine the structure of this net and, subsequently, it's programming.*

Personality is the indistinguishable ministration of reactive chemistry—an expression of intuitive equations that transmutes particle mechanics into fluid thought flow. Freed of all the universal laws of physics, bound by the catalyst of the present environment, the personality blooms as a natural, bacterial progression. A virus really, known clinically as imagination....

—Maybe our genes are out of sync. - my friend said.

—Is there a test for that?

—No...but I'm moving back in, for good.

—Shit.

His hands trembled above the coffee cup. —For as long as I can stand it...

My friend settled into the apartment, but he refused to get furniture. I was stuck with a bitter man and very few friends. Callet Street was filled with transvestites. They lived in basement apartments with lead-caked windows.

I met Shiva and Iona hanging out on the stoop. Shiva was lean and gaunt, with inflated balloon-like cheeks and one hell of an Adam's apple. Iona was rounder, hula-hoop thighs congealed into a fleshy, battery-packed mid-section.

They worked together, standing on the same corner, or on the same stoop every night. I bought them a few packs of menthol cigarettes and a six-pack of Wiederman's beer. We'd sit on the stoop and shoot the shit while they flagged down cars after the bars closed.

My friend was home before six. In the bathroom, I swallowed the last ounce of silvery liquid I had stashed in an old shampoo bottle. I walked down Callet to the spot on the corner where Shiva and Iona hung out. I offered:
—I got Newports, lights and menthols, I got Marlboro lights -
—Gimme the menthols - Iona answered
—I got some 100's too.
—Newport 100's? – Shiva asked
—Yeah. I handed her the pack.
—What the fuck am I supposed to do with one pack?
—Smoke them. I turned to Iona, —You want a Wiederman's?

—I don't drink beer, she said
—It was on sale.
Iona asked me, —You want to fuck us for a pack of cigarettes and a beer?
—Sure
Shiva's voice was flat, —You want to fuck me?
—Maybe later
They left me on the stoop and took off down Callet. I followed about twenty feet behind.

A bald man in a box-shaped car stalked us down Callet. He pulled up next to Shiva and said something I couldn't hear. Shiva tossed a lit cigarette in his car; he sped off cursing...*niggas...fucking nigga whores*.... Shiva turned around:

—You got anymore cigarettes...walker?
—No.

At the end of Callet, we turned east on Proctor Avenue. The Waterfront Boulevard was crowded with Chinese restaurants and sports bars. A plastic jitney pulled by a scruffy college student in a baseball cap zipped by. Three young girls with ornamental hair, wearing white plastic gloves bounced almost perpendicular to the street.

A few blocks down East Proctor Street, past a few shuttered ware-houses and grilled brick carcasses charbroiled and abandoned, we reached the point.

Officially, it was called Falsted's point, after a revolutionary war admiral named Falsted. Ninety percent of all the legal bars in the city were strung together along razor thin streets and piss-soaked alleys. College students roamed in single-sex coveys.

Shiva and Iona abandoned me on Helton Street. I found an empty barstool at Reston's Inn. The regulars were playing a card game called Tonk, a frenetic four-card poker. Hours passed as the cigarette butts piled high in plastic ashtrays. I finished off about three beers.

As I moved past the pool table to take a piss I saw Sarah, who was, unknown to me, hawking the pristine concoction that I would later learn was Orange.

Sometimes a person's aura can be infused with pure beauty and still end up looking odd. An extreme combination of physical elements can turn a face magnetic, her insulin skin, a cursive hairline... Sarah was out of whack, alienesque, freakish.

She spoke to a tall man in a wool suit and eyed me. She was black and white, or piquant gray, depending on the light. She crossed her legs as if they were armed and they were. She picked up a pool stick and struck the balls, visibly excited by primordial collisions.

I downed a shot of Citron before sidling up next to the table.
—Next game? I asked.
She spoke without looking at me.
—No, but you can buy me a beer.
—I don't even know you.
—If you don't...there are at least ten other men in this bar that will.
—Just ten?
—That's all I count. They all want to fuck me.
I said, —I know plenty of men that would fuck me; they wear dresses.
She turned in a circle, facing a wall of dyslexic pool cues. Her slender legs and rounded backside looked warm and inviting.
—Here, she said, choose a stick.
I grabbed a pool cue.

Her face couldn't be watered down by bar smoke. Her smile glowed through the light of a dampened lamp, the incandescent green that shaded the pool table and swallowed her eyes with an olive decay. Her breasts where small but accentuated by pronounced shoulders that expanded along a solid frame. She looked delicate but confident, a warmth offset by dark diamond-shaped irises. I asked:

—Always hang out alone?

—Not always.

—I'll get that drink.

I bought her the drink and managed to coerce her to sit in the closest booth next to the pool table. She stared at me, motionless mouth, silver-black eyelids. We sat silently for a while, then I asked:

—What's your name?

—Why do you want to know my name?

—If it's a problem, I'll tell you mine.

—I don't want to know...I want you to touch my face.

I reached across the table. The shadow outline of her face felt like mesh wire on the tips of my fingers. The sharp curve of her nose split her face in perfect halves.

She got up slowly, walked around table, sat down next to me, grabbed me by the back of the neck, and kissed me. I kissed back, measuring her face in the darkness. We kissed again, for an hour straight. She moved her lips from side to side like a child. I pulled her mouth into mine and tried to swallow her tongue.

I groped her body and she moved. Her breasts were inaccessible. I put my hands between her legs. She whispered in my ear, *not now, maybe some other time*. Pulling her body back, she rolled out of the booth and stood up.

—I have to go.

—Now?

—Yes now, wasn't that enough?

—How about a phone number?

—My name is Sarah, I'll find you.

Her name was Sarah. Sarah...I just remembered her name, mulling it over as I rode home in a cab.

...alternate route designated by
...a red signal, or ...system-wide emergency...(inhale)
...all auxiliary vehicles must be
...rerouted by auxiliary dispatch
...station by sub-controller
...during emergency...emergency power
...provided by auxiliary generator
...to be activated by the absolute indifference
...of a cellophane God...

The word processor hummed as the technical manual sank between my legs. The Turkish systems engineer slurred instructions through garlic breath as I tried to understand his thick, indecipherable accent.

...A level one emergency is indicated
... by a at least one triggered emergency
...signal; phase two, the safety
...sequence, is to be completed after
....all checklists from phase
...one have been approved by
...a qualified emergency engineer
...in codified sequence only to be written by the holy writ of wrap...

The clock turned over as an overweight data entry clerk at the terminal next to me grabbed a bottle of Liquid Paper off the table. She ducked under a desk, sniffing or snorting, coming up a few seconds later red faced and smiling.

—Try it, she said, laughing, holding out the bottle of white.

I ate lunch alone on a bench in the middle of Midtown Park Center, a paved causeway ending at Hellington Market. Indian hot dog vendors wearing cotton hats clucked in thick accents. Polaroid photographers sold prestige photos against the backdrop of a BMW or champagne bottle spray-painted on a sheet. I smelled Sarah in an unnecessary and abstract scent drifting from the office supply store.

That night I bought some beer for Iona and Shiva. We smoked a couple packs of cigarettes as the hot afternoon air rolled through the cataract alleys of Callet. As we drank, we talked about a maniacal stocking run that couldn't be fixed and the importance of clean needles (wrapped in warm plastic or tinfoil) and industrial strength rubbers. I ran down the block to the corner package store to get some more beer while Iona yelled:

—I'll fuck you up the ass honkey before you find a woman sweeter, fresher, and hotter than this whore!

No man is a man before he has a man that isn't, or a beer colder than a woman who is...

Sitting in the apartment a few days later, I played with the leftovers of mescan2, shooting it from the bottom of a glass of vodka. The apartment was empty, I was alone, my friend was off stalking Marcia.

Fading into the silence, the Mescan2 working it's way down the corridors of neural pathways that always settled on release, I felt the presence of someone next to me. Turning to look through my own internal light dimmers, my father sat, studying the glass that had just slipped out of my hand.

—You drink this shit, no wonder you can't get a job.

The soot lighting blackened his features. I opened my mouth to speak, but he interrupted.

—Don't speak, you've got no defense.

—Listen, it's not exactly my fault...

—Shut-up, I have something for you.

He reached into his shirt pocket, took out a piece of paper, and placed it in my hand.

Standing over me in a shadow, I noticed a small glint of silver lighting his eye sockets from behind. I said:

—I have to get rid of you if I want to leave.

—Of course, but you can't.

—Yes I can.

—No, you can't, unless you join me...

In the last minute before midnight, I slipped out of consciousness.

The next morning, I found Sarah's phone number written on a wad of newspaper stuck in the palm of my hand.

The point rests beneath a tidal wave of oil rush fog. I was sitting next to Sarah on a bench. Not a date, but a get-together I arranged because, I figured, my father gave me her number for a reason.
—I don't know how you got my phone number.
—Does it matter?
—I wasn't expecting to see you again, that's all
Sarah sat next to me on the bench, sipping a beer I bought at the liquor store on the corner. We watched the harbor lights blink like malignant stars, all out of whack and pulsating.

I turned my body, grabbed her shoulders, and kissed her. Sarah pulled her lips away, fixating on a tugboat mulching the oil-soaked harbor. I asked:
—Are you crazy?
She unrolled her skirt, placing it back over her knees.
—No, but you obviously are...
I grabbed her by the shoulders and kissed her again. She kissed back with fierce confusion and disinfectant clarity. Breaking it off, I said:
—Let's go to my apartment.
—Not tonight.
—Why not?
—You could be a freak.
—That's possible.
—Or poor.
I lit a cigarette. —And I smoke.

The tugboat took a turn, stirring the coffee thick harbor into the watery shoals of mescaline indifference. Sarah seemed as distant as fractal lights spread seamless across the water. Blinking in patterns I could not decode, the night faded into a brackish hue.

Wakeupwakeupwakeupwakeupwakeupwakeup...
My friend stood over me, snarling, as if I had slept forever. His
head was stitched with a wide seam, lower forehead around the side
of his skull, mapped with sutures. He was holding a duffel bag.
—Is that all you do is sleep?
—Only when I know you're going to show up.
—Wise ass.
He took the duffel bag and tossed it into the empty bedroom
—I'm back.
—Again? Is this final, like the last final time?
—Get off the couch dickface
—Fuck you, I'm tired.
—Get off my fucking couch.
I wouldn't move.
My friend dropped on the couch, I moved to one side. His tightly
controlled limbs sprawled in a Spiderman's pose. He asked me about
the pills I spilled in the sink.
—The sink is a mess.
—Yeah.
—What are those stains?
—They're mine.
—From what?
—Drink mixing...chemistry.
—It looks like paint not chemistry.
—Call it what you want, you drank it.
There were stains on the cracked yellow sink, smudges of blue,
green, and red.

Later my friend was primal screaming in the shower. I offered him my last bottle of Wiederman's beer. I grabbed it from the refrigerator and rolled it across the bathroom floor.

—Fuck you! He shouted as the bottle shattered against the door. After the shower, he sat on the couch in the living room and wiped the sweat off his eyebrows. He was perspiring like a large, heavy-coated dog. He mumbled something about Marcia between his cursing about our lack of air conditioning.

He mopped his forehead with birthday napkins sent by his mother. He continued to wipe his brow until a crown of paper spread across his forehead. Patches of white paper turned red with irritation. He wiped it again and again until the skin was almost purple all the while complaining:

—I'm sweating, I can't stop sweating.

—Stop worrying, it only gets worse if you think about it.

—Maybe we should get an air conditioner?

—And carry it out when we get evicted?

—We need something!

—I could borrow a fan from the guy downstairs, if you stop bitching.

—My scar really fucking hurts.

—Enjoy the heat. Summer's going to end sometime.

—It never ends here dammit, it hurts...

My friend got off the couch and walked to the empty bedroom. I overheard him dial the phone and whisper.

This time I call because I'm getting edgy. Whatever peace I'd found in the bowels of this apartment had been disturbed by Sarah's odd smell and my father's harassment. The only way to fight back was to slip into a prescriptive coma. So I called this time.

—Hey...wake the fuck up.

—What the hell do you want?

—Anything really, my friend cleaned me out.

—Jesus, it's late.

—There's a 'too late' for a fucking drug dealer?

I heard a match crackle. He took a hit off of something, and after exhaling, he said, —What do you need?

—The sedative stuff, the Exactilite, and more...maybe.

This time my father was watching TV. Sitting in a lawn chair, stroking his chocolate beard, his features colored black by the sky. I sat down next to him.

—You can't figure it out, son.

—What?

—How to get rid of me.

—No.

He laughed.

—We can leave together, if you want

—It doesn't matter.

—Did you see Sarah?

—Yes.

—She can get you out.

—Of what?

The black sky parsed in the middle, swelling up into a sort of fecal rain. Bridged by the gap of time between him and me, I saw the sun up-end a million graves, then dive into a pile of mulch.

I slept for several days after the late night visit from my dealer. Twelve doses of Electravite had produced a somnolent coma that helped me bypass my friend's crappy wake-ups, a few calls from the temp agency, and my dealer's seismic stereo. It was an empty, satisfying sleep that produced a sickening jolt of remembering her as I stared down the five o'clock sun beating on my puffed out, medicinal face. My friend was talking to me:

—I need the fucking rent.

—We're squatters asshole, we don't pay rent.

—I do, so pay it now; I'll hold the money in my account.

—You're fucking kidding.

—Somebody has to take responsibility.

—For squatting?

He paced around the television

—What the fuck have you been doing, do you have any jobs?

—Next assignment, you'll get all the money.

We both heard it simultaneously, loud footsteps on the landing. My friend shut up, ducking down behind the couch. Motioning towards the kitchen, I grabbed him by the collar and dragged him out of the living room. At the window, we heard the door opening. My friend cursed:

—The fucking landlord, just when I was getting things together.

—How do you know it's the landlord?

—Who else?

Climbing out of the kitchen window, I noticed the fire escape was truncated, blasted off at the second floor. No way down but to jump. A dumpster was within range, reachable with a little bit of

push off the end.   I said:
—C'mon, we gotta get down.

Jumping off the edge, my legs extended to hit the trash feet first. Landing square in the middle of the dumpster, I grabbed the side and braced myself.

Vaulting out of the dumpster, landing in the back parking lot, I turned around. My friend had crawled to one side of the fire escape, rolled up in a ball.
—C'mon, you gotta jump! I yelled.
—No fucking way!
—It's not that bad!
—Not into a fucking dumpster filled with fucking rats!
I picked up a rock and threw it at him.
—Hey...what the fuck are you doing? He yelled.
—You gotta come down, they'll find you up there!
As the second rock left my hand, my dealer appeared on the fire escape. He stepped back as the rock missed my friend, sailed past the dealer's head, and threaded the bars through the kitchen window. My dealer pulled out his gun and pointed it at me.
—You want to try that again?
—What the fuck are you doing?
—I got something new, but I don't know if I want to give it to you now.
—We thought you were the fucking landlord.
The dealer pointed his gun behind his back, smiled at me, and shot off a round.
—You like that?
—I'll take it.
I ran around the front and met him on the landing, pocketing two green pills and a good night's sleep.

The phone rings in the middle of my dream.

—Hello?

Recording: —Hello, this is the PermaTemp, voice-activated dispatch system. You have an assignment at 1522 Pulston Street, Vendrick Engineering, Fourth Floor. If you can accept this assignment please say yes after the tone...Please say yes after the tone...Please speak clearly...Please open your fucking mouth TEMP!

—Who was that? My friend asked.

—The temp agency, I've got an assignment.

—Good, get your ass off the couch.

—Can I borrow your car?

—No fucking way.

—You want the money right, you want me out of here, you want me gone. We'll lend me the car so I can at least earn bus money to get back to New York!

He studied me with two profane eyes.

—Alright, fuck it, go ahead.

Driving his Volkswagen Jetta down Callet, I decided to skip the conjured temp assignment. I stopped at the corner grocery and bought a few yellow bottles of St. Ides from an old Korean man with half a mustache.

I drove around for about an hour. Taking hits off the bottle, I got drunk and tired, so I parked on a sidewalk in the warehouse district.

It rained in uneven bursts, gently at first, then coming down in a deluge. I spotted two men dancing on the corner; the night had become vague.

The men were rolling full forty bottles down the sidewalk into a gutter, shuffling around in a little circle dance. One bottle would drop off the curb and shatter, and they would line up another and roll it down into the gutter. The cycle of destruction was repeated so many times that I wanted to get out of the car and ask them if I could drink the beer before they smashed the next bottle.

A heavy, richly curved young woman walked around the corner. She was dancing; her moves were ferociously sensual. Titanic hips that swayed unevenly and free with pleasure. Hypnotized by the massive fertility of the woman, so large but still mobile, I drifted off into a dreamless sleep.

When I got home the next morning, my friend was sitting in the
bathroom, slumped against the wall, sipping on one of my premixed
glasses.
—What are you doing? I asked, standing in the hall.
His wild eyes pulsed through the dust-filtered light.
—Marcia told me she liked it better, us living apart.
—That's her final answer?
—Yes.
—Wait, here, I've got something for that.
With agile hands and a sense that if I sent him down the wrong
chemical path it might soon be over, I reminisced a drink that
worked for me, Melancholy Billy: the mellowing effects of
methadone, without the physical limitations of pure dope. Greenish
clouds of powder floated through yellowish veils of wine. I placed
the glass in his hand. He took a sip, and his head rolled up back
against the wall.
—Why are you wasting your time? I asked.
He was rubbing his skull against the wall. —Who the hell asked you?
—You should have.
—She'll change her mind, come around.
—But you'll be dead.
—Not before I take you with me...
His head rebounded off the wall. He crushed his fingers into a ball
of spindly bones, cracking with percussive strength. —I'll never die.
Not now before you do anyway.

TOMORROW
PART THREE

The phone rings.

—Hello? Hello?

I was sitting on the fire escape launching beer bottles at my collective of rats, waiting for my friend to come home. Cardboard pizza scraps and molded cereal boxes compounded a valley of garbage that had run over the sides of the dumpster and spilled into the alley. I'd mixed a drink for him, a knockout punch that was sure to save Marcia the trouble of answering the phone.

It was Sarah.

—I need to see you.

—Sarah?

—Can you come over?

I was curious, but killing my friend was exciting enough to make me answer:

—I don't know.

—I need to see you now.

—I'm busy Sarah.

—You need money?

Temp assignments had been rare, and I was into my dealer for at least a c-note, so I hit the street to the address of a hotel Sarah gave me over the phone

Sarah opened the door.

A man was sitting on the couch, middle-aged, slumped in an arm-chair, legs stretched across a thick glass coffee table. He had deep pores and a tanned, bloated face. He wore bizarre flared jeans, a colorful shirt, and a black sport jacket.

Sarah led me to the couch. She wandered around the room in a semi-circle, pausing in front of the fabricated fireplace.
—How have you been?
—Alright.
The man on the couch spoke. —Who the fuck is this?
—He's the one I told you about, Paul.
Paul rolled his eyes. Sarah explained:
—I met him in a bar; he's been bothering me.
Paul said, —Do we have to do this now...
—Paul! Sarah interrupted. Turning to me, she asked, —Do you want something to drink?
—Yes.
She went to the kitchen to get the drinks. On the coffee table was a gallon-sized plastic milk carton filled with a fine orange powder. A plastic scoop lay empty next to a postal scale. Rows of round plastic dressing containers were stacked in small pyramids. A cigarette bobbed in Paul's mouth. I said:
—It looks like Tang.
—Well shit, aren't you bright. Sarah?
Sarah came back into the room with a beer in her hand.
—Yes, Paul?
—Who the hell is this?
—I told you already.
—Well...he's asking questions about...
He pointed at the orange powder.
Sarah feigned surprise.

—This exceeds my comfort level, Sarah.

—We need help, remember?

—I don't care, you know the rules.

She walked around the coffee table, took me by the hand, and sat down on the couch. Speaking to Paul, as soft as I've heard her voice:

—He's the best I could do .

—I don't care, he's an unknown, get rid of him.

Sarah hesitated. —He's harmless.

—NOW!

Paul's voice wrecked the quiet of Sarah's living room. She said to me:

—You have to leave.

—You called me.

—Forget it, you have to leave.

—Just because this asshole...

—Goddammit, leave!

Sarah was trembling. Paul slumped into the couch.

—I'm not leaving Sarah.

—You're leaving now.

She walked around the coffee table again, straddled my lap, grabbed my shoulders, and kissed me. I watched Paul fiddle with his cigarette out of the corner of my eye. I could smell it instead of her, burnt tobacco. She pulled off the kiss, took a deep breath, and purred:

—I'll meet you later.

I stood up. Paul's eyes were closed, the cigarette sat on his tie still burning. I got up off the couch, walked out the door, and went home.

—You don't think or fucking believe that I can't suck dick better than a woman?
—Are you saying you're not a woman?
It was hot and claustrophobic. Iona was sitting on the stoop, sculpting empty cigarette cartons. We'd drunk a six-pack of Wiederman's.

My friend had come home early and locked himself in the empty bedroom. I knocked on the door, he told me to go away. He called me an asshole. His laptop was vertical against the wall in the corner of the living room.
—Lipstick, perfume, mascara, they ain't never gonna care enough to ask.
—That doesn't mean I'm interested.
—Who the fuck is that?
Iona was looking out across the street. Sarah was standing next to a cab in front of my row house. I crossed the street to intercept her as she walked up the stoop.
—Coming to see me?
She turned around, cool balanced pivot.
—Paul wants to talk.
—He kicked me out last night, so fuck you both.
—Got anything better to do?
—Yeah.
—You need 200 dollars?
—Not really.

We took a cab to the hotel. In transit, she sat with her hands on her lap, looking out the window, humming a tune I didn't recognize.

I was into my dealer for one-fifty, my friend was bearing down for the rent. I needed money, so at the apartment when I was seated like a student in a small, uncomfortable chair facing the couch I didn't impulsively kick Paul in the balls. He was animated, talking a mile a minute while Sarah poured three glasses of wine.

—What's up Paul? You kicked me out last night.

Paul stopped talking and stared at me like he was pissed because I had addressed him directly.

—We're looking for assistants. Security, we need extra security.

Paul hiccuped as he pressed a wineglass against the end of his chin, Sarah spoke first:

—Paul is a professor of Anthropologic Postmodern Culture at Lasiterre University.

Paul finished off the glass of wine before speaking:

—This is my project, our project.

—Project?

—The distribution of Orange.

—What's Orange?

—A drug.

—You're drug dealers?

Paul laughed, flipping his tie over his back.

—No asshole, we're researchers.

—Dealing drugs?

—*Okay, even if I am always condescending it doesn't mean I have to give you some sort of patronizing, chemical rationalization of what we're doing here. Let's just say I have some theories, some universal theories of conscious-*

ness that go way beyond the pseudo science like that bastard Searle, and well, beyond the average buffoon layman like yourself. You see, knowledge is just an outgrowth of excess capacity for desire, and now that we've reached the postmodern graveyard, well, it's like flying in a holding pattern in a disintegrating jet. It's the unnatural magnification, the apportioning of energy to the point of nihilism. But you wouldn't understand this shit even if I spelled it out for you one syllable at a time.

Put it this way, if I had the schematic of the entire universe on the tip of my fingertip, I wouldn't be god, I would be observing matter in the transitional state, you understand, the transitional state. It's where everything gets ugly, where every molecule becomes a haze of misunderstanding...like every asshole on the planet cracking a textbook without picking up a pencil and doing the intrinsic math. What can you add and subtract in the nebulous, when in motion, going in reverse and forward at the same time...what the fuck is quantifiable about the flux? So you see, I have to do something to help people, I reveal the other side of understanding is the emotive power of transitions. So Orange, which is the fine sugary powder on the table is not an ordinary mind-altering drug. It's not about firing neurons and adding serotonin, it's about feeling the movement, the spikes of flux in our patterns of cognitive recognition that allow us to reassemble our existence not with systems but through Soul.
—Soul?
—Soul is the mirror that never transpires...I found Orange, that is, the substance. Let's say it was brought to my attention. Now it is in my care. It is orange, that's obvious. It is a project, a drug with a history context, but not a drug...understand? I'm sure you don't. I call it proactive, biochemical philosophical evolution. Distribution is, of course, the problem. Control is the science, the measured way of making it happen. I control, dole it out to the people with the right intellectual balance and give the rest placebos. I ask you, are you ready for, euphemistically speaking...a nuero-chemical makeover?.

Do you know what the fuck you're getting into? I can't change the aftermath.
After today, tomorrow, you might want your old state of mind back and
then...it's too late...
—So, it's not like heroin or cocaine? I asked.
—No.
Lifting the empty wineglass off his chest, Paul looked at Sarah who
quickly jumped up and took it from his hand.
—Couldn't you sell it in a drug store, Paul?
—We have to keep it in the right circles.
—Circles?
—Got to feel it out, test the waters...academic research son.
Sarah walked back into the living room, balancing Paul's brandy
snifter in the palm of her hand.
—Can we trust him? Paul looked at Sarah.
—Of course, Paul. He's in a coma.
I added, for effect, — That's her opinion.
—Good.
Paul stood up and checked his watch, then finished off his drink.
—It's almost time for the first round....
Sarah placed me in the shaded corner of the couch as Paul disap-
peared into the bedroom. She switched on the stereo, loading a CD
into a sleek black multi-changer. Pristine jazz melted from the large
speakers hidden behind two potted plants. She disappeared into the
bathroom while I sat on the couch.

Ten minutes later, she walked back into the living room. Her face
was sanded down with a thick layer of base, eyebrows rounded with
slick velvet paint. Her lips were parted with rose-colored lipstick.
She sat down next to me.
—What's in this for me?
—$200.

She flew off the couch and ran into the kitchen. The doorbell rang as Paul entered the living room sucking on a cigarette.

—Sit over there. She pointed at a chair in the corner.

Stopping at the door, she turned around.

—Ready?

Paul raised his hand in an inverted peace sign. Sarah opened the door. A middle-aged woman entered, dark hair pulled back behind her ears and a pair of sunglasses swung over the top her head. She was tall and almost too thin. A row of colored bracelets covered both of her arms.

—Are you ready? Sarah asked. The woman nodded.

—This way

Paul turned and headed toward the bedroom and the woman followed. Sarah closed the bedroom down, walked across the living room and sat down on the couch.

—I hate the interviews...but Paul insists.

—He's paranoid, you'd be better off dealing it on the street.

—Don't be stupid, this isn't an ordinary drug, it's Orange. She lit a cigarette.

—Orange?

—Yes, Orange.

Sarah got up and adjusted the volume on the stereo. She sat back down on the couch and adjusted her make-up with quick, agitated strokes.

A few minutes later the bedroom door opened. The woman walked quickly across the living room, handing a piece of paper to Sarah. Sarah ran into the kitchen and came back with a small plastic container of orange powder. She handed it to the woman, who bolted for the door.

Sarah whispered, — don't forget to return the feedback form.
The woman didn't answer as the door closed. Paul spoke, —I'm
going to wait in the bedroom.
Paul walked into the bedroom and shut the door. Sarah sat back
down on the couch.
—He gets a little testy when he's administering.
—Sarah?
—Yes?
—What is it?
She rolled her eyes. The doorbell rang again. This time it was a
balding, heavyset man bundled in a green ski parka. His face was
strained red; he had small peevish features between layers of
inflamed skin. Sarah led him to the bedroom. The door opened
and closed. I asked:
—How many tonight?
—Seventeen on the schedule.
The bedroom door opened. Paul shouted:
—Water!
Sarah bounced up from the couch, rushed to the kitchen, and went
back to the bedroom holding the glass away from her body like a
talisman. She sat back down on the couch.
—Paul is demanding.
—Yeah, but...
—Yes?
—What is it?
Sarah smiled, Licked her lips.
—Stick around and you'll find out.

At the end of the evening, after a dozen or so weary-eyed nonde-
script middle-class drug seekers had stalked the bedroom, Paul
handed me a wad of twenty-dollar bills. I counted two hundred

bucks, my total take for one week of temping before taxes. (He called it a stipend).

Paul said,

—Can you be here on Thursday?

—Sure.

Paul paced around the living room.

—I need the money, Paul.

—Good, but there are rules.

—What rules?

—Not now. He raised his hand with a fascist flair. —Sarah will explain later, you can leave.

Sarah looked worn out. I took the elevator to the lobby, hailing a cab as the sun turned on its side and slid though the canyon of terminated concrete.

The faucet opens. The sink explodes; the water is hot and magnetic. I rinse my hands, clean to the bones, remove bacteria with special caustic soap. I'm scrubbing and twisting, getting hotter and wiser, twisting the sun in my hands. It was the water, the color, the water and the color burning my hands, a solvent. Definitely, most definitely, I was turning Orange.

The natural rush of acrid gas from the raw, exposed end of a ruptured pipe blew an intoxicating breeze. Sarah sipped on a sixteen ounce I'd bought from the Korean. She watched as silent tugboats drifted into a dark blank horizon, slinking above the water.
—What are the rules, Sarah?
—First of all, Paul calls the shots.
—Yeah?
—Second, and this is the important thing, never try it yourself.
—Why fucking not?
—Paul's meticulous about dissemination.
—Meaning?
—If you try it, you'll fuck up the experiment, you'll fuck with the spread, the control.

The low-frequency sounding of a tugboat interrupted a long period of silence. Her beauty was unnatural; it was a concoction, the sandstone skin and freak eyes. I kissed her again. It was clinical and explosive. We had reached the limit, the exchange of saliva.

—Can't we get past this?

—Not now.

She laughed as her head rolled back up on the seat. Her left eye pointed towards a hovering helicopter, flush behind a mammoth smokestack. She took a deep breath and pulled my cigarette from my hand, then bent across the seat to whisper in my ear:

—I need to help Paul. Do your job, and you can have what you want.

— Alright.

—He needs to administer Orange, that's all we have to do...then we can fuck.

She laughed again, opening the car door and walking out onto the railroad tracks.

I was unraveled by her threadbare sensuality, her low-cut summer dress. A glass of scotch floated across the living room in her hand. Paul stood next to the bedroom door. Sarah asked:

—Are we ready?

Paul checked his watch. —The first interview is late.

The doorbell rang, and Paul extended his arm with an inverted v-shaped salute. Sarah walked the first applicant into the bedroom, then returned to the couch.

—Want something to drink?

—Scotch and soda.

Sarah returned with my drink. As she paced in a circle, I added a little powder from a small plastic bag stashed in my pocket. The polymer-like fibers were broadcast through the shards of sparkling soda and settled. I asked Sarah...

—So...what is it?

—HAVEN'T I SAID ENOUGH!!!!!!!! Paul yelled from the bedroom. He rushed to the center of the living room, stopping in front of the couch.

—*I have given you enough information, all the aspects of Orange, and you still insist on asking, like there's some sort of Magic School Bus theorem. It's bullshit, just bullshit, that Sarah has to sit here and suffer through your reductive, and I might add, incessant thinking.*

I can't fix your brain...understand. I can't fix your brain.

I can't make you think your mind is not the psychic center of the universe. It's just a random multiplier that expands reality along the infinite horizon called time. Of course, now we have machines that will do that for us, but still some of the residual instinct for being remains. Orange...Orange can get you there, or at least get you back...back onto the horizon...into the mix...how can I explain it, it's simple. People walk through my door, plead their case, and leave with pure, unadulterated possibility. They pay and I deliver. Consequently, I'm not buried in a pile of books in the university library of lecturing at another conference weaning an expense account and dreaming of sabbaticals. I'm just here doing what I do; Sarah is doing what she does. Why can't you exist for a moment and do your fucking job and stop asking questions?

—Paul, I just...

He raised his hand.

—Just be patient and I'll take care of you.

Five hours later I collected another two hundred dollars. My career as a temp was over as my shift as a bodyguard lasted into the hours slightly right of midnight.

Looking at myself in the mirror, I found my skin again too white. It was like ivory, a million suns too bright.

How long should I be passive living the mystery of Orange? Sarah's antiseptic mouth, Paul's unlimited vocabulary. It is not a matter of being honest or pushing limits or what is known.

I'm the dull bodyguard working for a dealer who is pushing a drug that could be a breakfast beverage. Does it matter? I wonder.

So the observer observes the observed and then what? Goes to sleep and waits to be called again? I wait for the phone to ring, that's my fucking job. I always answer it. The phone is my avatar rush; it's all that gets me out of the apartment.

Tomorrow I will find Orange on my own...

I culled the bars of Thomas Street. In and out, a beer or two. All the same, TV sets hung suspended in the dark wake of cigarette smoke. Cross-eyed regulars drank in isolating booths made of plastic and sand. I looked for signs of Orange, but found nothing.

Two blocks from the water-taxi dock was Jeremy's, my favorite bar on the Point. The beer was always warm and the bar food as inedible as the mold on the ceiling in the bathrooms. It was the last bar on the block, my final stop.

Taking a seat, I surveyed the crowd. A fat rectangular woman smoked a Tiparillo. Her jelly face seemed to roll down the sides of her neck. A skinny man with yellow fingernails dug through ashtray, laying cigarette butts across the bar in funky triangles.

The pool table, adjacent to the bar, was active. A large black man worked the table, sinking balls as he moved quickly from corner to corner.

Swigging off a beer that had been empty for an hour, he lined up the final shot, eight-ball bank in the side pocket. The cue slipped out his hand, knocking the eight ball off the table. It rolled along the bottom of the bar. I picked it up and laughed. He wasn't amused:
—You think that's funny?
—What?
—The way I play pool?

—It's not how far you hit it.

—Buy me a beer.

I ordered the beer.

His name was Ellis. He had deep-set eyes and a beard that rode down the length of his neck. His voice was deep and resonant.

I downed the citron, ordered another. Ellis lit a cigarette. I said:

—They say you know what's up.

—What the fuck do you know? He leaned over the bar.

—What do you got?

—Depends on what you have.

He drained a shot of Jägermeister, wiping his lips with the sleeve of his t-shirt. He said:

—Let's do some business...you need raw?

—No.

—I'll keep going...scramble?

—No.

—Fucking punk.

Smoke flushed from his nose.

I asked, —What about Orange?

—Where the hell did you hear about that?

—Doesn't matter, I know.

—You don't know shit, can't get it anyway.

—You could get it.

—I don't need it.

—Why?

Ellis laughed. Bared his teeth, chewing on the gummy leftovers of a cigarette filter.

—Believe it, I don't.

—Well I do

—It's gonna cost.

—Let's go.

Ellis pointed out a left turn, then a right. Through a dozen side streets and over a canyon sized pothole, I watched the city shift by through plate glass.

Ellis jumped out of the car and walked up the street. I parked and turned off the headlights, then turned on the radio, tuning it to a new and violent jazz mix show.

Paul was the prick that Sarah loved, and so I had the right to violate his rules. It's ridiculous, sitting in Sarah's living room, witness and protector of the administration without knowing. Orange, I could jump in the back seat and find out for myself.

Back on South Avenue, I pulled a credit card from my wallet. The edge became the scoop for the Orange powder that burned up my nose and spit brain cells into earwax.
—You want some I asked?
—Hell no. Like I said, I don't need it.
—I don't understand.
—You want, you don't know.
—Yeah.
—It's already up your nose, do you have to ask?
Ellis jimmied open the door of my friend's car with an empty beer can, he pulled his feet out into the street and sat facing the nettlesome, scuffed, star-lit skyline. Ellis said:
—Orange is soul.
—Soul?
—Sure, soul.
—I don't understand.
—Whatever

He watched me take another hit, bending his head towards the sky. Full of powder, my nose itched, eyes watered. The sky turned powder blue, the doors on the clouds opened up and dropped a bucket of rain on my head. Wetness behind my ears felt cool and refreshing.

—I can feel between the lines.

Ellis laughed, —Okay, it must be kicking in.

—It seems kind of funny.

—Not as funny as you.

I took another hit without hesitation. Ellis showed me his teeth before laughing it out.

—I work for the guy that deals this stuff, I mumbled.

—A great scam, a great fucking scam.

—I feel kind of in-between everything...

Ellis kicked the beer can out of the door and stepped in the car. — Let's get out of here before you get stupid.

2 4 : 0 1 : 0 6 : 0 8

The crowd jostled in the bowels of the humidified nightclub. An invisible DJ worked the mesmerizing, mechanical drum beat as the dancers picked up the response to some sort of nationalistic Beats Per Minute anthem.

Puerto Rico – Ho Party People – Ho White People – Ho Black People – Ho

I bounced between bodies like a pinball. I felt humble as I was tossed, punched, and shoved. The air was hot and suffocating. Smoke from pot fires scorched my lungs but I could, in fact, exhale. Ellis was standing on top of a speaker...

Puerto Rico – Ho Party People – Ho Puetro Rico – Ho Puerto Rico – Ho

Orange drove the epicenter of my buzz. I was connected to the beat, tangled in it. I could feel it prick my legs, work my spine, shuffle my internal organs. I could swing, move, project, and release at the right moment of every downbeat.

Two speakers larger than the Midtown Renaissance Towers shook with sub bass. The volume at my control...the equalization slightly altered by the power of my energized brain. *More bass...absofuckinglutley!*

Ellis pointed at me with his beer bottle. A young black woman with gravity-defying breasts stepped on my foot.

Puerto Rico – Ho Party People – Ho Puerto Rico – Ho White People – Ho

Outside the club Ellis said, —Maybe this shit does work.

—Meaning?

—A touch of flavor, I saw it.

—I don't know.

—Relax man; you're just as stupid as you were.

We walked back to the car. He pulled a tape from his pocket and popped it in the cassette deck. The bass drum rolled out behind a confused high hat. The first chord floated across my face...

My mind, just now and then wanders through the corridors and wonders what might have been...

Just as the tune stretched out into the humidified curvature of space, Ellis said: —Listen to it.

—I am.

—Listen...

—Sure, I am.

—No, listen like you want to.

—Jesus, I'm listening!

—No, move to it. If you ain't moving, you ain't listening.

Ellis nodded his head in sync, but not with every lagging kick. He dragged the dip into the next measure, smoothing out the transition between the organ and a backward rolling bass line.

—You'll get it, keep the tape.

—What...practice?

—Hell no, just take your time between the beats.

—Yeah.

—Orange or not, you can do it.

The woman from the club stood next to the passenger's side window. She raised her embroidered t-shirt. A pair of Machiavellian breasts lay an inch from my face. Large, luxurious nipples, perfectly pointed, majestic like a mountain range, perched at the fold of her taut, coffee-colored stomach. I rolled down the window and looked up. She said,

—Twenty bucks or my boyfriend will beat ya ass.

The best twenty I had spent to date.

Ellis was wiping lint off the windshield. Layers of cigarette ash had accumulated since last night. We were parked at the park. The neatly placed trees were separated by squares of sour grass. It was sometime the next day, late afternoon.
—Did the backdrop always seem so colorful?
—What? Ellis turned his head, rubbing his eyes with powerful fists.
—What are you talking about?
—The way everything seems behind everything that's in the foreground.
—Are you still high?
—I don't know.
Picking up an empty beer bottle off the floor of the passengers seat, Ellis jacked the bottle skyward, sucking the air out of it for a final sip. He asked:
—How can it look different than what it is?
—That's what I'm asking.
—Maybe you're hallucinating.
—I see the trees, the rich green leaves and then...
—Then what?
—Everything behind everything else.
—What?
—The colors.
—Yeah...you're high, on fucking what I don't know.
Later I dropped off Ellis and drove back to the apartment. I looked for the fly, but he was gone. Who else would understand? The phone rang.
—Hello? I heard Sarah whisper.

—Sarah?

—Please come.

—I'm supposed to be over tonight?

—I need you here now.

—What's wrong?

—I'm lonely.

This was before I picked up Ellis again and took a quick spin. Spin around the block and dip in the card under my nose.

—The thing about dipping, Ellis remembered, —is the needle kills. The rest is up to you.

I took that as sound advice before sitting through a seven-hour administration period during which Sarah got drunk. After more than a half-dozen citron shots, I asked:

—You and Paul are fucking?

—Sure...but we're not in love.

—Okay.

—Orange is our passion, not each other.

—Drug dealing?

—It makes everything better, even sex.

Sarah stood up, climbed onto my lap, and clawed me like a cat.

—I'll show you if you shut up...

She kissed me. A one-way lip fuck that put me into a one-way coma. Finished, she slowly slid off my lap, stood up, and smiled.

—Now, I shut you up.

When my shift was over, Paul handed me two hundred dollars with a firm handshake, followed by a cold, retreating smile. Sarah smiled too, devious but splendid.

The next evening, the phone rang. I had ridden another wave of
Orange with Ellis and was sleeping off an unnatural hangover.
Water was strange and indigestible. I settled down into the couch
and waited for my head to stop shrinking. The phone rang though,
and I was awake.

—Hello?

—Why aren't you here? It was Sarah. I answered:

—Paul told me to come over at nine.

—What happened to you last night? She asked.

I didn't remember. —I don't remember.

She sighed. It was my job to ask:

—What's bothering you anyway?

—I need to see you.

—At the apartment?

—Meet me on the roof of the hotel.

—Where?

—We need to talk.

I walked over to the hotel. A man in a wheelchair sat next to the
elevator as Sarah held it open with her leg.

—Hurry!

—What's the rush?

—We need to talk before Paul gets here.

She looked paler than usual. Riding to the roof, she said nothing.

The doors opened, we walked from the elevator to the terrace. I
looked over the edge of the crenellated rooftop. The city was just a
matter of angles. I offered her a cigarette.

—Are you okay? I asked.

—I'm fine, are you?

—Sure

Sarah moved towards the edge of the roof, turned quickly, and laughed.

—Would it be a surprise?

—What are you talking about?

—If I fucked you on the roof while Paul was out buying beer?

She threw her arms around my shoulders. My head bent into the soft inner curve of her lip. She pushed against my forehead, leaning into my body.

Suddenly, a pair of hands grabbed me around the waist and lifted me head first over the wall. Fighting back to regain my balance, another set of hands grabbed my legs and rolled me over the side. Before I could right myself, I slipped over the edge of the building, gripping the edge of the crenellate, dangling thirty stories above the sidewalk.

—Sarah! Sarah!

Paul's head appeared over the side. My legs kicked in a ventilating backstroke, clutching an abutment and scrambling for solid footing.

—Paul, Jesus, help me!

He bent down, his tie flapping in the wind.

—*You violate the rules. `Try it without asking. Use a goddamn sub-dealer and take a drug you couldn't possibly understand. Keep it in the fucking circle, I meant that. What did you want to know...about the spread, the control, the fucking methodology. Are you that fucking curious? KEEP IT IN THE FUCKING CIRCLE was meant to keep it simple for YOU!!! You betray Orange; the idea of Orange by taking it without proper administration...the whole process is adulterated by your ignorance. The simple mind cannot be SIMPLIFIED!!!! You're a parasite...a traitor...through your ignorance, this* *opportunity might be permanently lost...the experiment fucking RUINED, ALL MY WORK DOWN THE FUCKING PROVERBIAL DRAIN! You asked, what is it? Only a fool engaging in some sort of egotistical head-trip would want to know. What is it? Who the fuck knows...but it will kill you tonight.*

His tie lapped my face. My hands were numb, my body in shock stasis.

—*Orange is not a recreational high or a means to trivialize escapism. I am not an elitist...I didn't exclude you. I'm a pragmatist, in everything...and this first test of Orange will not be fucked up by morons like you taking my drug and dancing through an infinite happy hour!*

—Jesus Paul, could you lecture me later! I screamed. —Sarah, SARAH HELP ME!!!

Paul leaned back, his smile widened in the terminal breeze.

—Don't bother, this was her idea.

My hands were stone cold. Paul leaned over the fence again.

—It was her idea, maybe that'll give you a header.

—I'm sorry...I'M REALLY FUCKING SORRY!

—Too late amigo, you are going down.

—I saved your fucking life!

—GOODBYE! Paul's face contorted, screwed up, and twisted. He drew his head back, then sneezed downwind. At that instant, his tie was within reach, so I grabbed it.

Sarah's scream was on a rising scale, a terrifying crescendo. My leverage, Paul's body, the opposing force of his intellect bent on killing me and the bloodless hand gripping his tie put me one arm up on the fence.

I had enough strength to roll onto the terrace, while Paul dropped to the sidewalk. Concrete meets causality, a body fractured into dry pounds of flesh.

Sarah was laid out in a plastic deck chair, curled up in the fetal position. Paul was dead. I lit a cigarette.

There was a gathering of police helicopters a half a mile distant. Scattered beacons flashed agitated Morse code to the screeching cop cars below. A feline scream and the helicopters rolled out in a loose sortie, moving towards the rooftop.

I said, still shaking and wet with my own piss: —He wouldn't be dead if he'd stopped talking.
Sarah didn't answer. I continued....
—You guys are getting carried away with this drug-dealing thing.
—Shit, I don't know what to say, like COULDN'T WE HAVE TALKED FIRST!
Sarah was tight, sobbing, bound up, and useless. She screamed:
—We weren't going to fucking kill you!
I circled Sarah, pacing as I talked. She curled tighter, practically pushing her head through the mesh bands of the chair, sobbing and choking.
—Don't give me...don't give me the fucking academic subtlety shit. I'm too stupid to understand. I was hanging by my fucking fingers twenty stories over concrete! I stooped down to yell to the back of her head. —Is that it, the fucking subtlety I'm missing, the symbolism, the nuance...was it all a BIG FUCKING METAPHOR?!

I sat down, lit another cigarette. — Two fucking PhD's and you get this idea. Sarah turned her head and yelled, — Paul's dead you fucking bastard!

—It was self-defense. I answered.

—BULLSHIT, YOU FUCKING KILLED HIM!

—You want to call it premeditated?

—I don't give a fuck!

She looked at me; her face was pure porcelain lean, devoid of color. I said:

—We should get our story straight.

—Fuck you.

—You want to go to jail?

—You killed him.

Clutching her ankles, she started to rock slightly.

—The point is Sarah, everybody that knows you...knows him...and nobody knows who the fuck I am. Either way it's you or me or someone else...If we keep it straight, it's not us.

—I don't care. She started to cry again.

—Fine explain it yourself, the project too...

I walked towards the door. Sarah disentangled her slender body from the plastic chair.

—What do you mean, the project?

I ratcheted up the rhetoric.

—Orange dies with Paul, if you let it.

—Oh God....help me!

Stopping at the door, I felt the cold sensation of lust:

—Why? Why the fuck should I?

—You need the money...

Standing erect, her body poised again, the perfect breasts, slender legs all snapped back to form.

—It was your idea to kill me.

—Yes, but Paul talked me out of it.

I pulled her up by the shoulders, and she hugged me. I instinctively searched the terrace for other murderous shadows.

The cops stopped us in the lobby, and Sarah immediately started to cry. I stroked her stiff, sutured hair, massaged her tapered neck with my thumb and dropped my hand beneath the seams of her pleated skirt.

A fat cop with a coffee-soured mustache asked the questions. Sarah sobbed, alternately burying her head in my shoulder.

—You witnessed the deceased jump from the building?

—I describe it more like falling, I answered.

The cop paused. —You mean he didn't jump?

—It was awkward, but definitely a suicide.

The cop asked Sarah a question, —And you were there too?

—Yes.

He doodled on the pad. —Did you know him?

I hesitated, then answered, —No, we were just making out.

Sarah wiped tears with a bloodstained paper towel.

—He lived in the building Miss, correct?

Sarah's voice became dry and irritable. —I don't know.

The cop looked up at me and asked. —You live in the building?

—No. I answered.

—Have you seen him before?

—I don't know.

—Can't remember or don't know?

—I don't know.

The cop continued to take notes as Sarah broke loose of my grip and walked towards the elevator.

—I have to call my father.

The cop didn't say anything, continuing to write as Sarah walked away.

—You can go too.

I turned quickly, but the elevator doors were closed.

Taking the stairs to Sarah's apartment, I twisted the doorknob, but it was locked. I went home and described the night's events to a large, lethargic, and disinterested cat.

ORANGE
PART FOUR

A large pothole miraculously spawned on Callet Street. A natural crack in the pavement that swallowed a terminally parked car and became the final resting place of Iona...

He was taking a mid-afternoon nap when a vindictive gap, larger than any natural parting of pavement that I had ever seen, swallowed the car whole.

People rushed into the street panicked, like it was an earthquake. A DPW SWAT team in green fatigues swarmed the block, trying to dig the car out with an antiquated backhoe that broke down twice in a cyclone of hot ash and diesel fumes. After an hour, the work was called done, and a ton of recycled bricks were dumped to cover the gaping hole.

Out of respect for Iona, I held a memorial service. I placed the speakers from my friend's stereo in the window and read a few poems by Renaldo Arenas and sang two songs from Stevie Wonder's album *Songs in the Key of Life* while the other transvestites joined in with their unusually structured harmonies.

Good Morn or Evening Friends Here's your Friendly Announcer I Have Serious News to Pass on To Everybody
As a final act of remembrance, with respect and proper legal title, I named the pothole after him, or her: Iona. I painted it across the uneven pavement. It read: HERE LIES IONA, WHORE AND

FRIEND. BITCH, COCK SUCKER, DEAR AND BELOVED HERMAPHERDITE. The old woman wrote a one-line poem and read it with a dry beer voice:

—Potholes are potential in this city.

I thought, as Iona was laid to rest, that life is marked by turning points, especially a linear life like mine. I picked up the phone and called Ellis:

—Paul is dead, the Orange dealer I told you about.

—Shit, everybody knows.

—I killed him.

—Whatever...

—I know where he keeps it, the Orange.

—Now you're talking .

—Fucking right, it belongs to me.

On the way to Ellis' apartment, I considered how naturally every idea seemed to evolve from the starting point of death. If I could capitalize on his mistake, or at least prove his middling theories incorrect, the idea of escape would be resolved. I wouldn't need to justify loving Sarah, hating Paula, or moving to a hollowed out version of yesterday's city.

The door to Sarah's apartment was locked. Ellis threw his massive shoulders into it, knocking it off the hinges.

The apartment was dark except for a long line of evaporating candles on the coffee table. I saw the outline of Sarah glowing against the off-white shading of the couch.
—Sarah, it's me.
—I know.
Her body looked loose and scrawny. Dark shades drowned eye sockets into miniature caskets. She lifted her chin towards the ceiling and looked at me cock-eyed.
—You're not the first person who tried.
—Could we turn on the lights?
—No.
Ellis found the lights.

Lighted, her paleness looked death white. Her mulatto coloring drained, exhausted.
—Okay Sarah, where did he keep it?
—Not here.
—Bullshit, I saw it.
Ellis searched the bedroom and the closets. I opened every cabinet in the kitchen and fished through the refrigerator. After several minutes, I came back into the living room.
—Give it up Sarah, we'll find it.
—I told you, Paul didn't keep it here.

—Why waste it? Let us get rid of it.

—Fuck you, MURDERER!

...groping for inspiration, the indefatigable clue...a gesture...a memory of Paul doing something....

—TANG!!! I yelled the word with a force that jolted Sarah's head backwards.

Ellis answered, —Tang?

I ran into the kitchen and threw open the door of a small pantry next to the refrigerator. Rows of Campbell's Soup cans were stacked in a symmetrical wall. Cream of mushroom, asparagus, tomato. I knocked the cans backwards and sideways as Sarah wrestled with Ellis on the temperate linoleum floor. The wall of soup collapsed revealing another, more substantial pyramid of Tang. It was Tang, or labeled Tang, in large plastic milk cartons. Bulk Tang dressed with zesty orange and green labels. I picked up a bottle, fondled it, pulled the corner of the label off clean to reveal....

O	R	A	N	G	E
Soul		for		White	People

Contents: *Elaborate spices, crushed onions, real authentic sounds, alkaloid acids, and Orange dye no. 92.3*

Ellis had Sarah pinned to the kitchen floor. I yelled:

—We got it! We got a shit load!

—We got it?

—Enough to supply the whole fucking city!

Ellis lifted Sarah off the ground with a single, front-loading scoop. She lay in his arms, dangling loosely, speaking in tongues. I asked Ellis:

—Is she conscious?

—I don't know, maybe we should lock her in the bedroom.
—Drop her on the couch.
He carried Sarah into the living room, gently unrolling her body across the couch. I knelt down next to her head.
—Sarah...
She looked at me cross-eyed. I said:
—Sleep Sarah, you need sleep...
—Don't fucking touch it, don't take the Orange!
—I have to, it's mine now.
—You fucking loser, he's dead, it's mine, all fucking mine...
Ellis stacked the Orange in two cardboard boxes. I grabbed the top box and walked to the door. Sarah's voice followed me into the hallway:
—If you take it, I'll get you. I'll fucking kill you.
I took a hit scooped from an open container. I said with a smooth, electric simplicity:
—It's as good as gone...

Paul's failure would not be mine, so I consulted the only man I knew who would have an opinion about...

Distribution.

My friend's theory of distribution (categorized as, I know he was good for somethin'):
Market Driven versus Product Driven
Market-driven distribution: The drug is an established brand with widely recognizable benefits. Long history of use by a diverse and addicted customer base... Integral pop culture presence... Marketing strategies exploit slight pricing differentials, illusion of excess demand, and minor chemical improvements. Distribution should efficiently satiate demand on a wide-scale basis. Preserving or expanding market-share fundamental to increasing or maintaining profitability.
OR
Product driven distribution: New product with potential appealing properties and effects. Consumer demand and awareness almost nil, need strong hands on push to build brand awareness...grass roots focus, so I called Ellis:
—Street teams? I asked.
—Yeah, groups of cats that go out and make it happen...runners...punks that already have a customer base.
—You know some street teams?
—Yeah.
We returned to the block of my first Orange-colored experience. I parked the car next to a diminishing black alley. Ellis got up out of the car.

—Wait here.

He disappeared into a corner store. A blimp-sized cloud floated across the top of a ragged four-story apartment building; fog was migrating as transparent humidity out of the city. Ellis returned with a few young guys in long white t-shirts. He knocked on the driver's side window.

—Open the trunk.

I opened the trunk and got out of the car. Ellis was doling out Orange in small plastic boxes. The street teams studied the containers. Ellis spoke up:

—White folks, whatever, just remember it doesn't work...

One of the street teamers said, —Shit, I know the rules, whites only, ladies first.

They stuffed the containers into every available pocket. Ellis counted out fine-grained Orange to himself as he watched the gathering of inventory. He looked at me with appreciation as a gangly child-like boy with a barely visible face asked:

—What's your take?

—Nothing for now.

—Is it shit then? The boy looked skeptically at the powder.

—It's new; we need to break it first.

The street team sidled off into the wake of an approaching dusk. Ellis got back into the car and fumbled with a dangling seat belt. He talked with his hands, trying to conjure unintelligible thoughts and concrete expletives.

—Why the fuck shouldn't we sell it?

—Marketing, like you said.

—Bullshit, the drug's already got a buzz.

—I don't want to sell it.

—What's the pay-off?

I started to turn the ignition as Ellis ducked under the dash. He said:

—Five-O...

I was carried like a human shield through the lobby of the police station. Two sets of hands turned my shoulders as we navigated the building.

They both smelled like garlic. I was lifted off the ground, turning corners and taking elevators to floors and rooms connected by tunnels and narrow hallways. I was dropped in a small chair in a windowless room. A large light bulb was lifted over my head. Two men stood behind a table, smoking and pacing. One of them spoke:

—Answer the questions we ask, comprende?

—Sure.

—Did you kill Paul Terrell? I heard another, deeper voice ask.

—Who?

—Paul Terrell.

—Never heard of him.

—We have a sworn statement that you were a friend of his lover.

—Who?

—Someone named..., he picked up a piece of paper, —Sarah.

—Oh....

—You remember?

—I knew that Paul, not his last name.

One of the voices took form, exiting the darkness. He was a square, compact man with rutted skin and gold wire-rimmed glasses. He looked almost fifty, but his motions were agitated and chicken-like.

—Allegedly, he jumped off a building downtown.

—I know that.

—Do you think it was a suicide?

—He jumped off the building, what else would you call it?

—Unless someone helped him.

—Who?

—You, or her, or maybe both of you together.

—We didn't get along.

—Never fucked her?

—No.

—You were at her apartment two days before he died.

—We were friends. I tried to fuck her.

The officer moved in a little closer. —I'm Detective Rosisky. I don't fuck with people just to FUCK WITH PEOPLE. I ask the questions, you answer. It wasn't suicide...I figure either you or the girl killed him.

—She's a little nuts I interjected.

—Whatever asshole...Jealously and love are primal motivators. In my mind you're the prime suspect. If you confess now, we'll wrap this up, no more time under the hot bulb. If you FUCK with ME and LIE...you'll feel lucky sitting in jail.

Rosisky ratcheted up his intensity, piping expletives out of plastic red veins bulging from the neck muscles crouched beneath his jaw. Distributing Orange had stretched the color of my moods, alternating free-form shapes that could be measured against any sort of intimidation. I raised my hand to request a moment to speak. Rosisky waited...

—Go fuck yourself Rosisky.

—What?

—I want an attorney.

—No.

—You don't have shit, nothing on me.

—I'll kill you, I swear to god, I'll fucking kill you!

Rosisky jumped around the table and lunged at my throat. A tall, mountain-sized black man with wild gray sideburns grabbed him by the arms. I waited for him to fold, but he was tireless. He yelled until his face turned red. Finally, his partner pulled him back into the corner. I couldn't see past the shadows but I recognized the undertones of strategizing. Finally, the larger cop spoke to me:

—You're the prime suspect, for now.

—I didn't kill him.

—Got an alibi?

—I was there, you know that.

—Stick around, don't leave town or we'll have you locked up.

—Can I go?

—If you can walk.

I didn't wait for an escort. I was out of the police station and into the beginning of tomorrow.

Back at the apartment, in the middle of an unbalanced sleep, my stomach finally exploded up the back of my throat. The pill (Electravite) had clashed; it was not in sync with other methodically smooth liquids, and I was sleeping off the edge of a terminal past. Dredging up conferences of color and pliant space, I was hypnotized by a spinning carousel of light my father had rigged up with a broken lamp and a rubber band. He filled the kitchen with flecks of electric paint, insane sparklers.

I steadied his hand with mine. He raised his eyes towards the ceiling. I wanted to say something that would make him listen to me. His hand rattled out of my grasp as we continued to spin, his light in motion, he said:
—I don't remember you being this ambitious.
—About what?
—Orange.
—Was I ever lazy?
—No, just undisciplined.
—You're mocking me.
—I'm remembering you, and hoping.
—That you'll be able to escape ?
—I can't leave, you know that son.
—I mean escape like me...
His confident spin unwound. The lights traced intricate patterns, frozen, static, indelible. I waited for his image to fade, the end of the dream. I could control it...I could shut it down...I turned off

the lights and left him in the dark.

The phone rang.

—Hey, man.

—Ellis?

—What happened?

—It's all about Paul.

—Shit...do they have anything?

—Nothing, until Sarah talks. What's up with the street teams?

—Little nibbles, not much yet.

—We need promotion.

—Like what?

—I got an idea...

Asleep again, resting in the crevices of the couch, I turned my back, placed my hand on Paula's arm, and pretended that I cared enough to straighten the inward curling filaments of her hair. My father again, bothering me in a dream, this time in the kitchen digesting a dozen quick shots.

—You think you can ignore me? He asked.

—What are you talking about?

—I want to know what you're going to do.

—I told you, I can't....

I hadn't noticed the drink in his hand. It was Diet Coke but it wasn't. A tall sixteen-ounce shiny, colorful, cylinder of something...a faded label, a talisman...

—What is it? I asked, studying the drink.

—My own concoction.

—Is it good?

—No, idiot. He waved his hand. —The real question is: does it work?

—Does it?

—Better than anything you can imagine.

—So...

—Taste it.

He slid the can smoothly across the kitchen table. It rotated as it moved, a slightly metallic kaleidoscope phase...not completely solid until it stopped, inches from my hand. Reformed in the haziness of my dream, it resumed a cylindrical shape, buzzing like a satellite. I hesitated:

—I don't know.

—It's not a matter of understanding, do it.

—Yeah, but I'm not really asking you...

—Drink it before you wake up...it goes down easier...

On the couch the hour is drawn because the clock on the wall does not move. Small tufts of cat hair roll like tumbleweeds. A bitter salt paste coats my tongue. My hair is wet. I feel fully hydrated. It was spring water really, cold and reminiscent.

In the gray middle of a rainy afternoon, the sky drops below the clouds. A truck rolls up on its hind legs. The old woman reappears. A transvestite stretches after a long afternoon nap. The beer is cold. A cigarette tastes like breaded paper between my lips.

I think about this time, this time, how murky it was, why? Because I was caught in the middle of asking and answering, caught in-between the shade and contours of my shower. Water sparks snap me awake. The phone calls were constant. I was ingesting power. Getting into all the fucking madness and annihilating Orange with my nose. It was a new type of freedom, without concept, without an idea. Just move, move, move through the morning, pick at the sun and toss it in the garbage.

I left the bar to catch a beer and a smoke on the corner.

Ellis showed up, walking across the old bridge where I stood. We said nothing, walking together down the street until we reached a dead end at the gates of an overrun cemetery.

Taking a left, we made our way through a back alley to the doors of a Korean grocery. I bought a couple of beers, and Ellis bargained for his daily afternoon litmus snack.

Outside, Ellis swatted a gnat off his neck as a garbage truck weighed into the curb. Smog blew off the highest shot tower. I thought...*here is where the world turns upside down*...then Ellis took the cap from my beer and offered it to the Sun Goddess before packing it with ice. I asked him:

—What do the Gods want with that?

—Just letting her know I'll share if she asks.

Ellis lit a cigarette. —So what's your big idea?

—A party, an Orange party.

He laughed. —Whatever.

—Like the club, the night I tried it.

Ellis paused to consider, I kept talking.

—The music, the vibe, we need lights, it's gotta be atmospheric.

—Man...it's a big maybe.

—There's no risk, we'll just wrap the whole thing up...

—Finish it?

—The distribution of Orange.

—In one night, we'll make all the loot?

—Tie everything together.

Ellis looked at me expectantly. —So...

The phone habitually rings. It never used to. I've developed the habit of not answering — of letting it ring until it rings right. Until it purrs rather than moans, until it's in tune with the tremblers that rock my aching head.

I answered.

—Yes?

—Hey man, I got the flyers and the invites.

—Yeah.

—Shaped like twelve-inch labels.

—How many?

—10,000, three different colors.

—We're the street teams then.

—I'm ready, I need the loot.

I rolled away from the phone to find a fresh place to puke. On my hands and knees staring at the carpet. I dug my fingernails into the wall, rocking back and forth to restore bacterial equilibrium.

I hung up. It rang again. Outside the streets roiled with heat circling in a cyclone of hot ash and dust. The air was knotted, dirt molecules sat on the door frame. The phone kept ringing, so I answered.

—You can't ignore me.

—Sarah?

Her voice sounded friendly and calm, —I want to see you.

—No. I answered.

—You stupid shit. Her voice modulated through a bad connection.

—Where's Paul's orange?

—I gave it away.

She shrieked, —You gave it away!?

—Almost all of it.

—But it belongs to Paul!

—He's dead.

—You can't, you can't do this!

—He's dead Sarah...dead, dead, dead.

—It's still his.

—I'll save a little, send it in the mail.

—Fuck you, you fucking murderer!

I stuffed the receiver under a pillow on the couch.

Iona's pothole was dormant when I dropped the bottle into a small opening that had widened since the day of his memorial service. A wave of shattered glass trickled down the spout. I watched the last bit of booze melt away and cursed my luck at having only brought one bottle to the tomb of the well-known transvestite.

I stroked the bituminous grooves. The pitted sedimentary sheet of clay, asphalt, rock, and garbage compressed into a single strain of soft, molted rubber stretched out to meet my fingers across the divide of hardened tar.

As I was meditating on Iona's contours, a shadow cut across the tomb.
—Where the hell have you been, shithead?
It was my dealer. The half moon circles under his eyes now double tracked. I said:
—I've been sleeping.
—That's not the rumor, at least not the hot rumor.
I got up and stepped back, he wasn't a vague menace.
—I was going to call. I could use a few Electravite.
—You're fucking with me.
—Give me twenty dollars worth.
The Tech Nine was unsheathed from his crotch.
—You gotta ask permission to become a dealer on my block.
—Dealer?
—Everybody knows, man-fucker.

I tripped on the curb. My dealer pointed the gun at me.

—You can't just go and fuck up my business.

—I'm a loyal customer.

—My stuff is patented; I eat it, then pee into a cup, and mail the pee to myself. Anybody asks I open up the package and do the chemistry...it's my intellectual property.

—Okay.

—You're sampling me, asshole, without permission, like all those other ass-brained rappers that can't play a note.

He was standing in the center of Iona's tomb. Pointing the Tech Nine directly at my head, he smiled:

—I told you to get a gun.

—I'll buy that one.

—I'm sure you would....

Iona opened up, or, more accurately swallowed. The earth turned over in the maw of Gaia's gaping mouth, a vortex of bricks, mortar, paving, sucking like an inverse tornado.

In an instant my dealer was vacummed into the ground. Buried up to his head as the fractal paving shifted, turned over with an earthquake trough, then reassembled and froze into a sedimentary grave.

He was trapped, wide-eyed and scared, buried and immobile.

—Jesus Christ! Holy fucking shit! Help me! I can't fucking move!

My dealer twisted, thrusting his shoulders backwards trying to raise his arms above the hole.

—I gotta go. I started to walk away.

—What the fuck do you mean you gotta go! I still have my gun pointed at you!

Wild-eyed, full of fear, my dealer shrugged his shoulders, after which, I could swear I heard the muffled report of a gun.

—You like that asshole?!

—I'm late. I've got business to take care of.

—You are a fucking dealer...you muthafucker! You muthafucker!

Walking back towards the apartment, the muffled gunshots continued until a cloud of smoke drifted over my back.

—Hey! Fuck you! Get me out of here...get me out of here! Please...

Ellis called me on a cell phone. He was walking but pretended to be in a car. The ear shattering white noise spit through the receiver into my head. I could barely make out a complete sentence as Ellis worked to exaggerate:

—I think they're starting to bite.

—Yeah?

—We're halfway through the first box.

—The party is gonna work...just save the last box.

I hung up the phone before he could protest and waited for my ears to settle down. I laid my head down sideways on the couch, I was dreaming of water and residue, color, and incidental hygiene.

My friend left a letter addressed to me sitting on the couch with a note about my unpaid share of the beer stash. I wasn't surprised to see it had already been opened. I waited until it was dark and the TV purred with magnetic silence to read by the light of a brewing cigarette.

Inside the envelope, I found a news clipping:
LASITERRE PROFESSOR'S DEATH STILL SHROUDED IN MYSTERY

The death of Paul Terrell, the renowned professor of Anthropological Psychology at Lasiterre University has launched a full-scale homicide investigation. Initially ruled as suicide by police investigators, Prof. Terrell's fall from the roof of the Avalon Hotel is now termed "suspicious." Suspects, including a former lover of Prof. Terrell's, are now being sought for questioning.

Prof. Terrell's passing is being called "a tremendous tragedy." Acting provost of Lasiterre University, Michael Ebdecott, termed Terrell's death as "unexpected," adding, "Whenever a tenured member of the faculty departs the college prematurely, we feel unlimited grief."

Prof. Lasiterre was best known for his work on anthropological psychology, including a seminal anthology of urban linguistic semiotics titled "Primitive Celestial Speaking, the Language of Alternative Societies in America." His groundbreaking paper on the philosophical discourse in Amazonian societies, "Intuitive Practitioners," brought controversy and academic celebrity to Prof. Terrell. He was awarded the E.J. Browser Award for his book *Standing on a Stone, a hypothetical dialog with inertia.*

On the corner, we dropped off some invitations for the street team. Ellis launched into a stilted inspirational speech, but the hype was not needed. They'd made a few bucks, the product was taking off, and the party was the right coalescence of love that Orange needed to be a big hit. Everything was electric until Officer Rosisky drove up in a black, late-model Cadillac. He rolled down the window and yelled:

—You wanna talk here or in jail?

—Here.

—Let's go, asshole.

Back at the station, it was darker than I remembered:

—Who are you to ask questions? Or ask anything about what we're going to do with a scumbag drug addict like you. Who the fuck are you to ask us anything other than if we feel like cutting a deal? We're tired of fucking around. If you don't want to confess, maybe we'll put super-conductive battery clips on your balls...*or should we try your asshole*...or were you thinking we couldn't do that because it's not in our fucking budget. You're in a backwards-fucking city asshole, and one thing we have plenty of money for is to keep sadistic fucks like me happy. Understand? Comprende?!

Rosisky screamed until his face turned red. He sat down and took a sip from a coffee cup. I was staring out the window through the after burn of a hyper-hot day wondering why he didn't just ask or why I didn't just tell them.

His partner stood up and walked around the table. He leaned on my back and gripped my shoulders. Rosisky said something under his breath; I noticed a glint of silver cupped in his hand.

—Hold him down.

Quickly another cop was in the room. A near ton of weight fixed my arms on the table. Rosisky paced in front of me, clicking a small pair of nail clippers.

—I'm gonna clip your fucking nails.

He pounded on the table with his fist and laughed. The nail clippers rattled in his hand like animate silver teeth. He pulled on my thumb, then cut off the end of the nail, scooping the clipping in a small plastic bag with his free hand.

—Tie fibers...we find any and you wish you made a deal...we know the whole fucking story, every detail.

He was precise, almost methodically obsessed, clipping each nail until the soft tissue of my fingertips split. Each clipped fingernail was lovingly swept into the bag while I bled. Finishing my last finger, he stood up and examined the contents, small consulate fossils, while I bled all over the table.

—We've got you, this is it.

—Tie fibers?

—Exactly scumbag, tie fibers, crystal-clear evidence.

Rosisky circled around the table. I grabbed the chair and held it in front of my body. I dodged a couple of punches and ducked under a few roundhouses until his partner grabbed my arms and held me upright. Sparkling moments of pain, a brittle fist connected with my jaw, my ears started to ring. I smiled as his hand connected with the wall.

—Fucking punk, how'd it feel?

I didn't answer.

—How'd it fucking feel?

—I'm crying already.

—Give me a minute and you'll be shitting out your ears!

He hit me continually for a half an hour, stopping only to catch his breath and light another cigarette. I concentrated on Orange, the residue still flowing in my veins. Without it, the pain might have felt worse.

The bus rolled down Callet and toward Midtown Center. Ellis was tossing invitations out the window like Frisbee graffiti. I stuffed them into gummy seat corners.

Ellis sat down next to me and worked his large hands over the pages of a Keats anthology.
—What happened to your face?
—Rosisky.
The bus moved slowly down Callet, stopping to pick up a passenger. A tired old woman wrapped in cheap scarves slowly plied up the stairs, dropping coins in one at time. I said:
—We need a DJ, a system, big speakers...
—DJ B Shit, Ellis answered.
—Is he good?
—Hell yeah!
—DJ B Shit then, and a big system overlooking that park, from the parking garage, at the hotel.

The bus stopped on the corner of Sage and Wesley. We got off and walked past a crumbled service bay and onto a bridge overlooking a dissected highway. Ellis leaned into a wind that rippled through flaps of his loose-fitting turtleneck.
—How about this? The whole concept, DJ B Shit, free Orange, and...we sell t-shirts?
—Sure, Ellis.

Ellis couldn't find anything good from his regular mini-mart, nothing Orange, nothing red. Nothing colorful, like basic neon. I wanted day death; I needed Orange, but got a healthy wad of seething green.

Morning felt better than I expected. Natural drugs give smoother hangovers. That morning was as clear as any morning I could remember.

A tiny slice of blue sky threw unprocessed sunlight onto my block. Garbage was uglier in a natural light. The dullness of everything clean confuses the senses. Luckily, we rarely saw our block in this light.

Taking the phone off the floor, I floated onto the couch and placed the call I planned out the night before.
—Hello? I heard a soft voice collapse.
—Sarah?
—You. Was all she could manage.
—I don't like the way we left things.
—Really?
—How about dinner?
—When?
—Tonight.
—Yes.
—Yes? Okay, how about seven?
I hung up. It was the easiest date I'd ever made with her. It just had to go right.

If Sarah could do anything, she could wear a dress. Every dress she owned she wore well. And I'd never seen a skirt that didn't look

great on her legs. Not tight mini-skirts but knee-length sophisticat-
ed drapes that accented sleek length instead of compact muscle.

She walked towards my car, moving her shoulders forward, her hips
shifting provocatively along a precise line.

We drove to the Korean store in my neighborhood. I bought some
beer and stashed it in the back seat. I slipped a tape in the cassette
player and waited for Brother Isley to sing. Sarah inexplicably
smiled.
—I like this song.
It played on and got unnecessarily melancholy before I found a spot
near the warehouse. I parked the car and cracked opened two
beers. She took one and smiled:
—I like this spot...it's you.
I turned up the stereo and the conversation stopped. We finished
our beer. I wanted it to rain. She picked at a stocking run thread
loosely around an almost bare kneecap. I grabbed the empty beer
bottle from her and threw it out the window. I needed to know:
—What's your deal with the cops?
—You're assuming...
—I'm assuming they found me because of you.
—You don't know that.
—You tried to kill me.
—You killed Paul.
—It was self-defense, but we've had this argument.
Headlights swung around the corner. A car stopped in front of us, a
few feet away. I could see Ellis in the front seat lighting a cigarette.
I got out of the car and met Ellis halfway. He was dragging on a
butt with close determination. I asked:
—What now?

—Kill her.

—I don't know.

—She didn't hesitate to do you...it's what you have to do, if you're a drug dealer.

Street teams have street prescience and an incomplete working knowledge of police procedures. That's why, as Sarah got out of the car and raised her arms in a strictly mechanical motion, someone had the presence of mind to yell:

—GUN!!!

A bullet flew into the desert of mangled concrete. Another round pierced the windshield of Ellis' car, spraying shards of glass across the front seat. Before we could react, Sarah got off another round that skipped off the street and vanished into the harbor.

Retreating, we threw our bodies at the car as it locked gears and jumped backwards. Another shot pinged melodically as it skewered a stripped-down van. We reached the car and jumped through the open back door. The driver wrestled the steering wheel, righting the car away from Sarah around the corner. Ellis shouted:

—Jesus man, didn't you pat her down!

—I didn't know she had a fucking gun!

—She tried to kill you once, are you fucking stupid?!

Ellis rolled down the window as the car bounced on the cobblestone side street. We fell forward like weightless astronauts as it raced through a red light. I slumped down in the back seat and lit a cigarette and wondered if Sarah would ever get the job done right.

—I tried it; actually I'm on it.

—You're kidding.

—I bought it from a transvestite.

I never thought my friend would get Orange. He sat on the floor in our living room, hands folded over his knees, rocking like a toddler, humming a tune I didn't recognize.

My friend's face was slack and then quickly tight, his lips stretching back in an indefinite line around his skull.

—I feel edgy and then realized.

He lay down on the floor and closed his eyes. Suddenly his legs rose inches off the ground. I asked:

—What are you doing?

—Leg lifts.

—Mind if I smoke?

—Yes. Sit on my feet.

Lying flat on the floor, my friend went canine, rocking up and down, bouncing off the floor, staccato sit-ups. Timing the inhales, I made sure to exhale in his face whenever possible.

—Watch the fucking smoke!

—C'mon, relax. I decided to ask, —How's Marcia?

The true test: would Marcia survive the Orange gambit. My friend acknowledged the name with a contorted face; he rattled his knees like cartilage drumheads and rolled onto his back with his hands extended towards the ceiling.

—Marcia...ha! Fuck Marcia!

—Now you're talking.

—Raw bitch

—You're making sense.

—Can't say why I feel this way...I'm singing better too.

The tape replayed in an auto rewind dupe. The same song, Ellis' pick. My friend stood up, arms at his side, wired to the ceiling. He flopped around the living room to the beat, stamping the floor on the downbeat and raising his arms like a fascist referee on every chord. He sang:

—Looking down the corridor and wonders what might have been...

He stopped singing, —I think I have it, it feels intuitive.

—You're borderline palsied.

—No, no, this is fun.

—I can't watch.

—This is beyond everything, this is real life man.

—Real? You're real?

He fell to the floor. His arms maintained their upright, u-shaped position. His manipulated movement, off the beat, a pre-mortem stress reliever.

I stood up, walked towards the door thinking...*Orange could really be dangerous...in the wrong hands...maybe Paul was right...too late...*

I only read a few articles. I hadn't really slept in a week, so words were separate and hard to digest. A flow of phrases, however unclear, translated over several days into my assumption that something was happening.

MIGRATION BACK INTO THE CITY TIGHTENS RENTAL MARKET...LAKE TROUT, NUMBER ONE BISTRO DELICACY...B.E.A.T. RADIO SURGES TO NUMBER ONE...TWELVE-INCH VINYL, EVEN THE WHITE FOLKS ARE BUYING IT....

Ellis called me early that morning to break the news.

—That's it, we're through the first box.

—Good. Hold out until the party.

—Can't we sell a little?

—No.

—What about Sarah?

—I took care of it.

—How?

—Don't sweat it, just meet me at six.

—Make it five, DJ B Shit is setting up around then.

—Got it.

—Out...

I lied. Sarah was still at large. I couldn't kill her, and I didn't care if she wanted to kill me. I was bent on throwing a really good party. That would be the best finality begets a final sort of statement.

—Do you think you have enough juice? DJ B Shit looked up from a spaghetti pile of cables.

—I got 12,000 watts of power. He answered.

—And the lights?

—Outdoor amphitheater quality.

—You got the record I asked for?

—Yeah.

B Shit was a compact, muscular man. He moved with athletic ability, shuffling from amplifier to mixer to turntable with electric bursts of agility. Wires like magnetic crossroads covered the exposed top of the Mt. Avalon Hotel parking garage. DJ B Shit's road crew assembled a tangled sculpture of ornate lighting trees and speaker stacks.

Imagine a perfectly positioned podium, a floating platform hovering above the park. Sight lines, sound trajectories form a perfectly symmetrical relationship with the crowd assembled below. I picked it for symbolic reasons...I wanted Sarah to know.

The park was a wrought-iron shoe box. A grassy oasis surrounded by double-lane city streets and pulverizing bus routes. Smack in the middle was the statue, the horse without a rider.

I practiced the words in my head to maneuver around awkward sentences and unnecessary pauses. Preparation couldn't neutralize my nervousness. There was fear that we wouldn't draw a crowd, the anticipation of stepping off the threshold of change. There was the unresolved matter of Sarah. I knew that it may or may not happen: the scenarios were real and unarticulated. I was ready to throw a party.

Now the question was answered...incredibly simple, to think of it now. How could I respond to something, a color? I could wake up and everything would be forgotten. Or I could fall asleep, and wait until tomorrow to forget again. Ellis asked:

—Did you know it was going to take this long?

—What?

—To find out what it was?

—I had to pass it by a few times.

—Maybe you should keep moving.

—But I can...

...imagine the way the world is, which if other more lucid versions don't conform to what I'm seeing, can't be my fault. Maybe I imagined everything senseless, or just will it to be so. The point is I had forgotten enough soul on the way to Orange to remember how little it mattered. If it was a drug, and the drug was useless, if it was just a means to be inventive, then I say that's enough. I accept it, as it is, refined sugar, and recall my actions as real information, a true narrative. I employ situations to realize sadness, to make the mark of an unreasonable body. If I am upended by fact, then I will end on this note: The situation often is, or always is, less concrete than that on which I walk.

Ellis was decked out, wearing strong cologne. He looked happy, almost euphoric.

—I'm ready man, really ready.

—Where's the fucking crowd? I asked

—Here in a minute.

—You have the stuff?

—It's ready to go, wrapped, and portioned .

—Let's do it then.

—Alright...

The park was quiet, almost empty. We hung around smoking ciga-
rettes while B Shit rummaged through his record collection. He
asked:
—The first record?
—That anthem thing.
—I'm not getting it.
—Sing Sing beat?
—Okay...with the party chant.
—That's it
Ellis offered up a few bottles of bourbon, so we started our own
party, a few quick shots thrown back to heat our blood a little. Ellis'
cell phone rang. He looked surprised and handed me the phone.
—It's for you...
I knew without asking. My father had gone mobile.
—I'm going to be there, he said.
—I'm not surprised.
—I said some nasty things.
—Sure, but I understand now.
—I'll be wearing the usual...just be ready.
The line went dead. I drank another shot of bourbon. I tossed back
a succession of shots in marvelous quantities that wound around the
tip of my glass.

Soulful crowds congeal instantly. The party was a bust at 10:30. At
11:00, it was overflowing with bodies, white bodies restlessly scour-
ing the park for hidden caches of Orange. Ragged vendors selling t-

shirts and incense camped out around garbage pyres, screaming out prices, threats, and advice.

The crowd rearranged itself like a single organism; fractal patterns emerged as signs of intuition and energy. Diamond packs of women, loose gangs of men, all white and having a good time.

I walked over to where Ellis was standing and grabbed the microphone from B Shit. Ellis signaled to the street team, which retrieved the stash and fanned out along the edges of the building. I spoke first:
—White people...Orange addicts...
The crowd continued to hum. I went on:
—White people...ORANGE ADDICTS...party people, insomniacs, and burnouts...leftovers and all assembled unrepentant crackers, if soul is what you want then we got it...we fucking got it. PAY ATTENTION AND LEARN!

A beat dropped by B Shit rolled the speakers, a quick hit from a throbbing 808 kick. The crowd shut up. I raised my hands towards the bloated half moon.
—To the unfeeling...the cynics...if SOUL is what you want, we GOT IT....THE REAL EMOTIVE POWER IS HERE, UP HERE AND WAITING FOR YA...

B Shit set off a barrage of beats. Shots of substrata bass rolled waves of motion across the kinetic, swarming crowd. I walked to the edge of the building, raised my hands, spoke the words, climbed the summit, and unleashed the frustration and power of being:
—Puerto Rico!

I threw the microphone forward, waiting for the response. Silence.
—Puerto Rico!
Silence.
—PUETRO RICO!
Swallowing the mike, left arm extended in the air, I yelled again:
—Puerto Rico Ho!
Ellis stuck with me, leading the call with precise, distorted bursts,
taking over the call and response, adding a little improvisation:
—ONE MORE TIME! I CAN'T HEAR YOU! PUERTO RICO
HO! BLACK PEOPLE HO! WHITE PEOPLE HO! ALL PEO-
PLE!
ONE MORE TIME!
PUERTO RICO HO! BLACK PEOPLE HO! WHITE PEOPLE
HO! ALL PEOPLE HO!

B Shit threw scratches off the turntable. A violent wall of sound
burst into a frantic rhythm of double-time kicks and ferocious bass.

The crowd, stirred by the rush of sound, throttled into suddenly
realized energy, picked up the instinctual punctuation of the vibe.
Thousands of hands were raised as the street teams began to dis-
pense. My arms too were raised above my head...I had surrendered
as the street teams chucked plastic balls of Orange into the mass of
spare body parts. I began to repeat the anthem again.

The shot was amazingly in time. It came on the downbeat of the
first measure of a raw bass line. B Shit ducked, Ellis hit the deck,
and I turned to see Sarah holding a gun. A monumental silence
jerked the crowd. The sunset was suddenly a presence, colorfully
inert. I wondered at the colors, the sunset and the skyline, orange

and malevolent purple, patrician green and vertigo yellow. Swirling combinations that lingered, saturating the horizon with indefinable hues...Prozac azure...the sultry electricity of now.

A miracle shot, I thought, as I watched the bullet soar across the sky. Floating like a bird, soaring circular, spectacular patterns woven between the clouds. Would it hit me, attack like a vengeful insect? Was I scared? Should I duck?

It had a different agenda, not interested in killing me, flying to the sun, into the majestic dusk. Not getting involved, the merciful bullet with other purposes rocketed up towards the stratosphere, the orange sun and yellowish GOODBYE. I turned around...

A man held the gun up, twisted Sarah around, and pulled it from her hand. DJ B Shit bounced up and started scratching. Ellis raised his head, got to his feet, pulled up the mike and yelled:
—ONE MORE TIME...PUERTO RICO!
I left my perch and walked to Sarah's discarded body. Standing over her, his face smoothly shaved, glazed by the heat, my father smiled. He motioned with his manicured hand, motioned for me to come.

His skin was dark, porcelain, and sanded by time. I walked in a straight line past the street teams, B Shit, Ellis the newly minted rapper, the virtual sun, a trace of quiet traffic, the wild applause of an inebriated crowd, the carcass of Sarah, the emerging column of unshaven cops lead by Rosisky who yelled as I passed by:
—Lock this place down, lock it down. I want them all put away!
I walked past my friend, still righting himself, Iona and Shiva floating like helicopters, the coiling after-light that swept the roof with an Orange brush. The image of Paula, the image of the palace of

New York, the city streets deserted after five, and the sweet fragrance of Appleton's rum washed down with a hit of Electravite. I walked past everyone as Orange emerged in the bowels of the crowd and a sense of soul boiled over in the heat and into the palm of my quivering hand. I walked into his stride; we cruised on ice to the perch and watched...

In the frenzy, the street teams had abandoned the plastic, tossing Orange wholesale.... small clouds of condensed artificial color hovered over the park. Ellis remained on point, still riding the beat. It was a structured vibration, bodies that trembled in time and seemed to move up and down with sexual energy. It was not an addiction, as Paula predicted, but a simple, viral release. It was the end of a day. It was a celebration at the very least. It was something other than I could have imagined. It was something, definitely. I said to my father:
—I finally did it.
—Are you ready?
—Yes.
We laughed, and then I think we walked off the edge of the roof together, joining the party in a semblance fall.